When Santa Fell to Earth

When Santa

Fell to Earth

CORNELIA FUNKE

Translated by OLIVER G. LATSCH
Illustrated by PAUL HOWARD

SCHOLASTIC INC.
NEW YORK TORONTO LONDON AUCKLAND SYDNEY
MEXICO CITY NEW DELHI HONG KONG BUENOS AIRES

First published in Germany as *Als der Weihnachtsmann vom Himmel fiel* by Cecilie Dressler Verlag
Original text copyright © 1994 by Cecilie Dressler Verlag
English translation copyright © 2006 by Oliver Georg Latsch
Illustrations copyright © 2006 by Paul Howard

Published in the United Kingdom in 2006 by The Chicken House,
2 Palmer Street, Frome, Somerset BA11 1DS.

ISBN-13: 978-0-439-92301-9
ISBN-10: 0-439-92301-8

12 11 10 9 8 7 6 5 4 3 2 1   6 7 8 9 10 11/0

Printed in the U.S.A.   23
This edition first printing, November 2006

The text type was set in Clois Old Style SB.
The display type was set in Nicolas Coch SB and Swank.
Book design by Leyah Jensen

For Rolf

Also by

CORNELIA FUNKE

Contents

Niklas Goodfellow Falls to Earth

O n the tenth night of December, a terrible storm was approaching from the north. A thousand lightning bolts skewered the stars, and thunder rolled across the pitch-black sky with a sound like a derailed freight train.

Niklas Goodfellow, a Santa Claus by trade, didn't notice any of this. He lay fast asleep inside his caravan, snoring peacefully, while Twinklestar, his reindeer, pulled him through the clouds high above the sleeping world. Lightning licked the ramshackle caravan like a snake's tongue, but Niklas dreamed of almonds and marzipan, as Santas usually do.

Twinklestar galloped faster and faster through the black clouds. Still he could not outrun the storm. The rumbling darkness swallowed the stars, and lightning crackled between his hooves.

Terrified, Twinklestar reared up, broke his reins, and bolted down toward the Earth. Niklas Goodfellow's reindeerless caravan swayed from side to side like a boat on a churning sea. Then it toppled forward into the swirling clouds. Niklas tumbled out of his bed, hitting his head on the leg of a chair, and rolled helter-skelter under the table.

"Whoa there!" he shouted. "What's going on?"

But by then he and his caravan were already plummeting toward the ground.

Niklas's ears roared and his head reeled as if it were going to explode. The wheels of the caravan brushed against some treetops, bumped against a chimney, tore off a few TV antennae, and then landed with a crash in the gutter of a narrow street.

A flock of carrion crows rose from the branches of a bare lime tree, cawing angrily. A fat gray tomcat nearly fell off a roof. And the people kept awake by the storm thought: *What a thunderclap!* As though the moon had dropped from the sky.

Niklas Goodfellow's caravan rolled a little farther, then it leaned to one side with a groan and stopped.

Niklas took his hands from his ears and listened. No more roaring and raging, no crashing – only the rumble of thunder. He crawled from beneath the table. "Matilda? Emmanuel? Are you all right?" he called while he felt for his flashlight in the dark. But of course it was no longer where it had been before. Nothing was in its place anymore.

"Oh dear, oh dear! Oh dear me!" someone twittered. "What happened, Niklas?"

"If only I knew!" Niklas replied, gently prodding the huge bump on his forehead.

A match flared in the dark, and a small, plump lady angel fluttered down from the cupboard with a candle in her hand.

"Gracious me, what a misfortune!" she fussed, fluttering anxiously around Niklas. A second angel peered in shock from the edge of the cupboard. The young Santa was still sitting on his bottom, dumbfounded — in the midst of scattered books and broken crockery.

"Matilda," he said, "could you please check on the elves?"

"Oh, them!" Matilda put the candle on the table. "They're all right. Can't you hear them swearing again? Ugh!" There was a commotion in the top drawer of the upturned dresser. Excited voices were shouting over the top of one another.

"Yes, yes! I'll let you out," Matilda shouted back. "But first you must stop swearing. Otherwise I won't lift a wing, understood?"

Niklas rose and staggered across the tilted floor, toward the caravan door. Cautiously he peered out into the night. No living thing was to be seen. Yawning, he put on his red coat and climbed down the two rickety steps, almost tripping over a bent street sign that poked out from underneath the caravan. MISTY CLOSE, it said. "Blast!" Niklas shook his head. His caravan was leaning precariously into the gutter, two wheels broken.

"Look at this!" He sighed. "Aren't I the lucky one?!" And his reindeer was nowhere to be seen, either. Which was no surprise. All Christmas reindeer are invisible – but greedy, too. Niklas took a few bits of gingerbread from his pocket and held them out hopefully into the darkness.

"Twinklestar?" he called out quietly, clicking his tongue. "Twinklestar, food! Now come along, you faithless nag."

Nothing. No clattering hooves, no bells, no snorts. Just one last roll of thunder. A raindrop landed on Niklas Goodfellow's nose. *Splash*. The very next moment it began to pour, and Niklas stumbled wearily back into his caravan, while the rain poured down onto Misty Close so heavily that even the crows sought cover in the bare trees.

The Wrong Street

It was cold inside the caravan, so cold that Niklas
Goodfellow's breath hung in the air in white clouds. But
Matilda was already firing up the small stove, her wings
and her nose black with soot. Emmanuel was busy gathering
up the shattered crockery from the floor — tiny plates,
cups the size of thimbles, and scattered amongst
them the large broken pieces of Niklas's coffee mug.

"Misty Close," he murmured, lifting the top off the
window seat and rummaging around inside. "Now
where is my street map, for goodness' sake?"

The dresser was still shaking with the sounds
of tiny thuds and crashes.

"Matilda, have you still not let
those elves out?" asked Niklas.

"Well, they haven't stopped swearing yet!" Matilda answered defiantly.
"Isn't that right, Emmanuel?"

The other angel nodded. He was just as fat as Matilda but his head was bald, with a crest of silver curls around it.

"Oh come on, let them out," Niklas said. "Aren't we in enough trouble without your constant quarreling?"

Without a word Matilda slammed the stove door shut, fluttered over to the dresser, and tugged open the drawer. Out burst three dozen tiny men wearing red caps. Muttering and cursing, they jumped down onto the floor, clambered up the table legs, and inspected the damage from above.

"Booger-burps and reindeer poo! What kind of a mess is this?" cried the largest of them. "What happened?"

"We've fallen from the sky again," said Niklas wearily, and bent to look under his bed, but the map wasn't there, either.

"And where have we landed this time?" the elf asked.

"My dear Rufflebeard, that is exactly what I am trying to find out!" Niklas answered. "But I can't find the map!"

"Would it be the official Santa District Map you're looking for?" Matilda asked.

"That's the one."

"Well, why didn't you say so?" With an air of great importance she fluttered up toward a large basket that dangled from the ceiling and pulled the map out from underneath a pile of used ribbons, stale gingerbread men, and candle ends.

"Thank you." Niklas spread the map out on the table and

leaned over it anxiously. The elves crowded around him and the angels perched on his shoulders.

"Oh no," muttered Niklas. "Oh dear!"

"Smelly goblin farts! For once can't you just tell us what's going on?" grumbled Firebeard, a spindly elf with shaggy red hair.

"Well, that's rude!" Matilda leaned down from Niklas's shoulder. "You just mind your language, will you?"

The elf poked his green tongue out at her.

"Oh, stop it!" Niklas was still frowning at the map. Emmanuel shifted nervously on his shoulder. "What color is it?"

All the streets on the map were clearly marked in red, yellow, blue, and brown.

Niklas sighed. "Brown."

"Oh, steaming reindeer poo!" Rufflebeard shouted, stomping angrily all over the map.

"Rufflebeard, less of that swearing! That's no way for a Christmas elf to talk."

Niklas bent down, pushed aside a few tattered books, and carefully picked up a small machine.

"The snow machine," he mumbled, holding the device to his ear. "Broken as well. Not a sound. And where are the glowworms . . . ?"

He looked up at the ceiling, where countless luminous

spots were flickering in the dark. "Emmanuel, Matilda, could you please try to catch them? And you lot" — he tapped one of the elves on his cap — "will have to help me take off the broken wheels and repair them — tonight, if possible. The quicker we can get away from here, the better."

"Ech, yuk!!" In a flash all the elves had vanished underneath Niklas Goodfellow's quilt. "We're going to sleep," one of them croaked. Niklas just shook his head, but Matilda flapped her wings angrily.

"Well, if those aren't the laziest, rudest elves ever to be born in Yule Land . . ." She gasped for breath and nearly fell over.

"Don't be too hard on them, my dear." Niklas yawned while he swept the elves out from underneath his quilt. "After all, they do build the most wonderful toys, don't they?"

Cold air rushed in when he opened the caravan door; rain was still pelting down. The two angels, shivering, peered over Niklas Goodfellow's shoulder. A few of the elves bounced down the steps and started kicking around in the puddles.

"Not very Christmassy weather!" Emmanuel observed.

"You could say that again." Niklas sighed. Then he pulled his hood over his head and set to work with the elves.

The little fellows were hardly bigger than a coffee mug, but together they were stronger than most humans. Effortlessly they jacked up the caravan on big wooden blocks, unfastened the broken wheels from the axles, and pulled them off. Niklas hardly had to lift a finger. But when the elves had finally dragged the wheels inside the caravan, they were all so cold and drenched that none of them felt like fixing anything. So they hung up their wet clothes next to the stove, slurped some of the hot soup the angels had prepared, and crawled into their beds.

Soon the only sounds in the caravan were the crackling of the wood in the stove and the drumming of the rain on the roof. Niklas snored into his pillow, and in the big dresser drawer one of the elves swore gently in his sleep.

The Bet

I t was still dark when the first children came past
Niklas Goodfellow's caravan. Every morning hundreds of
them filed through Misty Close, heading for the school
at the end of the narrow street. It wasn't raining anymore,
but it had grown frosty overnight. A thin film of ice covered
the puddles and crunched under the children's feet.

Ben was trudging along the pavement with his friend
Will. He had crawled out of bed only half an hour ago,
because he lived very close to the school. But as far as Ben
was concerned it was still far too early. Why couldn't
school start at a decent hour — ten, for instance?
Ben sometimes thought his bad grades might
be just because he had to get up so early. . . .
Well, probably not. At least when it came to
sports, everyone wanted him on their team, but
as soon as a teacher asked him to talk instead
of jump or throw, he was lost. He wasn't any
good with words. They slipped from his tongue

the moment he wanted to say something. And so Ben mostly stayed silent.

"Look at that strange trailer," Will said, stopping in front of the caravan. "That wasn't here yesterday."

"Nope," said Ben.

"Looks like it's from a building site or something," Will observed. "Look, it's missing two wheels."

"Too colorful," said Ben.

"What do you mean, 'too colorful'?"

"Too colorful for a building site."

"Maybe it's from the circus. Or belongs to gypsies."

Ben shrugged. He thought the caravan looked strange somehow. Different. But as usual he couldn't find the right words to explain this to Will.

A few boys from their class passed by. They were shouting and pushing one another into the wet hedges, but as soon as they saw the trailer, they stopped. Dean, the math genius in Ben's class, was one of them. Dean was a master of words. And Dean was a real joker — at other people's expense, of course. That didn't make him very popular, but even the teachers respected his sharp tongue.

"Hey, Pea-brain." Dean shoved Ben with his elbow. "Did you park that heap of junk there? Planning to move out from your parents'?"

The others laughed.

Will tried to drag Ben away. But Ben didn't feel like leaving, and when that happened no one could move him. Especially not his friend Will.

Ben didn't like Dean. He didn't like him at all, and he would have loved to give a smart reply, something that would have made the others laugh at Dean for a change, but he couldn't think of anything. Of course not. So he just stared angrily at the bully.

"Uuuuh! Look at him. OK, I give up!" snorted Dean, pretending he was shaking with fear. The others cracked up.

"You know what I think?" Dean gave Ben a nasty smile. "I bet you're too chicken to go and knock on that door."

There was a tense silence. Will was still pulling Ben's arm. A woman walked past with a huge dog. The dog sniffed curiously at one of the colorful wheels, then peed on it. Ben looked up at the red door.

"Come on. I'll let you copy off me on the next math test," Dean teased, "if you knock and stay in front of the door until someone opens it. What do you say?"

That was a tempting bet for someone like Ben, who got massive headaches from just looking at numbers.

"OK, deal!" he murmured.

Will let go of his friend's arm, and the others immediately moved back a few steps to be out of the danger zone. Ben wiped his cold nose with his glove — and ran. He jumped up the caravan steps and knocked on the door. Once. Twice, as cool as possible, while his heart dropped into his boots.

"Now stay there!" Dean called from a safe distance. The others giggled nervously.

Ben stayed, for a whole clammy eternity.

Then suddenly the door sprang open. A tall young man smiled down at him.

"Yes?" Niklas Goodfellow asked.

"Morning!" Ben jumped down the steps again and ran off, pulling Will with him.

The others followed, whooping. Only when they had nearly reached the school gates did Ben slow down. Will was panting heavily, and even Dean was gasping like a beached fish when he finally caught up with them.

"Jeez, Pea-brain, what's the hurry?" he puffed. "That guy didn't exactly look like a cannibal. Or did you see anything else in that caravan?"

Ben shook his head sullenly. "Nope. What should I have seen?" Then he turned around and marched through the gate, Will in tow.

"So . . . *did* you see anything in there?" Will asked him in a low voice.

"No," Ben replied, avoiding Will's curious glance. What should he have answered? That he had seen a minuscule man with a red cap peering out of the man's coat pocket? There were no words to describe that.

A Visitor for Niklas Goodfellow

Niklas was sitting at his table sipping coffee, nibbling gingerbread, and mending a hole in his Santa coat. It was already dark outside. A whole day had passed and still only one of the broken wheels was leaning, fully mended, against the wall. The elves were still hammering away on the second one. And they were cursing. Of course.

"How is it going, Fuzzbeard?" Niklas asked, trying to thread his needle.

"Not good!" the stoutest of the elves answered. "I think we're going to hammer our fingers into smithereens on this one."

Niklas put down his needle with a sigh and looked at his coat. It was old and threadbare and covered with patches. "Matilda, could you thread this needle for me, please?" he asked. The two angels had been baking gingerbread and spiced biscuits all day.

"Just a moment!" Matilda wiped the flour from her hands and fluttered over to the table.

Niklas got up and walked over to the window. The lights of the city colored the night a smeary gray, and it was once again raining, a fine drizzly rain. On the other side of the road stood a small forlorn Christmas tree in front of one of the houses. The electric candles shimmered weakly through the drizzle, when suddenly Niklas saw the boy. He was standing next to a tree, behind a parked car, chewing on his thumbnail, staring at the caravan.

"Matilda, look!" Niklas said, surprised. "Isn't that the boy who knocked on our door this morning? What do you think? Should we ask him in?"

"Oh yes. How nice!" Matilda clapped her hands. "We haven't had a child visit us in ages."

The elves were distinctly less enthusiastic. "If he stares at us all the time, we kick him out again," one of them muttered.

"Exactly!" giggled the others. "*Boom* — and out!"

"You are really the most dreadful creatures!" Matilda

scolded. "There'll be no gingerbread for you, not a single piece. Understood?"

"Oi, hold on a sec!" The elves threw their hammers to the ground. "We work, we get gingerbread. 'Understood'?"

Niklas was still looking out the window. *Children are the best cure for Santa sadness*, he thought. *And Santas are good for sad children. So . . .*

"I'll ask him in." Determined, he walked over to the door and opened it. "Good evening, my friend!" he called. "Would you like to come in for a bit?"

The boy ducked his head and looked around. He took a couple of steps toward the caravan — and then one back. "Dinnertime," he muttered.

"Ah yes, I understand." Niklas nodded, disappointed. "Your parents are waiting."

"Oi, shut that door!" the elves shouted from inside. "Our fingers are freezing off."

The boy peered past Niklas into the caravan.

"Hello there!" Matilda flew onto Niklas's shoulder and gave the boy her most angelic smile.

"I — um — I — I'll just ask — my parents," he stuttered. Then he turned and ran across the street toward one of the garden gates.

It didn't take him long to come back.

Matilda was making hot chocolate when they heard the knock on the door.

"Come in!" Niklas called. He was still mending his coat.

Hesitantly the boy stepped into the caravan. A small music box stood on the table, tinkling a Christmas tune, but the elves had vanished.

Niklas pushed out a chair. "Do sit down. Matilda is just making you some hot chocolate. You do like hot chocolate, right?"

The boy nodded and picked up a tiny shoe from the chair. He placed it on the table as carefully as if it were made of glass and sat down. Emmanuel brought him a bowl of gingerbread, smiled shyly at him, and then fluttered back to his baking tray. The boy stared after him, his mouth wide open.

"What's your name?" Niklas asked.

"B . . . Ben."

The large dresser by the table started rattling.

"Oh, just come out!" Niklas called. "Does the boy look like a spy?"

"Those silly elves keep seeing spies everywhere!" Matilda said as she placed a steaming mug of hot chocolate in front of Ben. But the boy's eyes were on the tiny men, who were climbing out of the dresser's bottom drawer.

The largest one hopped toward him and stood right in front of his left shoe. He crossed his short, stout arms and glared at the boy suspiciously. "See, Niklas?" he said. "The human is staring at us. *Grrrr!*" The tiny chap made a face and poked out his green tongue.

Ben gave a start.

"These are my Christmas elves," Niklas explained. "I'm afraid their behavior isn't terribly polite. But they don't really mean it, right, Rufflebeard?"

The elf was still scrutinizing Ben.

"He looks too stupid to be a spy," he finally observed. Then he turned around and strolled back to the others, who had started to bang at a large wagon wheel with tiny hammers.

Ben stared into his mug and shyly took a few sips of Matilda's hot chocolate. He almost choked when the carved gnome standing next to the sugar bowl made faces at him.

"Those elves are so impertinent!" sighed Matilda, sitting down on the edge of the table. "Just ignore them. How do you like my hot chocolate?"

Ben nodded, staring at a small nutcracker stalking around stiffly on the top of the wardrobe.

"Not much of a talker, is he?" one of the elves called. The others giggled.

Ben turned as red as a Santa's coat.

"And what a nice change that makes!" Matilda shouted angrily at the elves. "If you kept your mouths shut more often, there wouldn't be so much trash coming out of them."

"Will you stop it, please?" Niklas moaned. "I wouldn't be the least bit surprised if our guest wanted to leave right now." He turned to Ben. "I really must apologize. Sometimes I think they just enjoy arguing. By the way, my name is Niklas Goodfellow. These are Matilda and Emmanuel and those badly behaved elves are called Specklebeard, Coalbeard, Goatbeard, Firebeard, Fuzzbeard, Rufflebeard, and so on. I have to admit, sometimes even I forget some of their names."

Ben nodded, still taking everything in.

"Have you noticed something?" Niklas asked.

"It's bigger inside than . . . than on the . . . outside," the boy stuttered.

Niklas smiled. "Exactly. All real Santa caravans are like this."

"Santa?" The boy looked at him incredulously. "Santa caravan?"

"Yes." Niklas milked a small wooden cow Matilda

had placed on the table and poured the milk into his coffee. "I am a Santa Claus. Yes, I know" — he stroked his stubbly chin — "I don't really look like one. I'm still quite young for a Santa, but . . ." He pulled a white woolen beard from a drawer underneath the table, hooked it behind his ears, and slipped into his threadbare red coat. Then he got up and pulled his hood over his hair.

"Does this look more like it?"

Ben nodded. His eyes hung on Niklas as if he were seeing him for the first time.

"Isn't he the most wonderful Santa Claus?" Matilda piped up. "The most wonderful of all!"

"Yes, the wonderfullest Santa of them all," sneered Rufflebeard, throwing his hammer into the corner. The elf hopped onto the table and planted himself right in front of the startled boy.

"The angel is right — for once," he whispered. "Forget about the rest, Niklas is the last true Santa. But if *that lot in there*, behind that door, had their way" — Rufflebeard pointed to a white door at the opposite end of the caravan — "our dear Niklas would have been turned into chocolate a long time ago."

"Oh be quiet!" cried Matilda, while Emmanuel covered his face with his wings.

"Well, he's right, Matilda." Niklas took off the white beard and hung his red coat over his chair.

"Why? Who's behind that door?" Ben asked anxiously, and stared at it. The door was barred with three strong bolts in the shape of pine-cones. A bell hung from the handle, and an elf boot was wedged into the keyhole.

"It's not a very nice story!" Niklas said. "Are you sure you want to hear it?"

Ben nodded, his eyes still on the White Door.

"OK then," Niklas sighed, "if you're sure." He sat down again and crossed his legs. "Maybe it's time to tell at least one child what really happened to Christmas."

The Great Christmas Council

"Two weeks before last Christmas," Niklas began, "the weather was as wet and icy as today, and I caught a terrible cold."

"Terrible indeed!" Matilda twittered, taking another piece of gingerbread. "He was sneezing constantly. The whole caravan shook."

"We were just wrapping a few Christmas presents," Niklas continued, "when suddenly there was this knock on the White Door."

All eyes turned toward the bolted door. Only Niklas kept staring into his coffee mug.

"It was a giant Nutcracker. He ground his teeth and grabbed me by the collar, announcing that the Great Christmas Council had summoned me."

"The Great Christmas Council?" Ben asked.

"The gathering of all Santa Clauses." Bugbeard made a disgusted face. "But only one of them has any real say there — Gerold Geronimus Goblynch.

Ever since that scoundrel has been in power up at the North Pole, Christmas has turned as sticky as honeyed toast!"

"Oh, that Gerold is such a creep!" Matilda shivered. "He bought snowmobiles for all the Santas and turned the reindeer into salami! He convinced most of the other Santas to forget about the children's wish lists and only take orders from the grown-ups — against advance payment, of course. And on Christmas Eve they deliver everything at the press of a button."

"Terrible!" Ben mumbled.

"Terrible?" screamed Rufflebeard. "If you think that's terrible, just listen to this. This is our new Christmas anthem. Gerold composed it himself." He grabbed Niklas Goodfellow's spoon and swung it like a walking stick while he tap-danced across the table and sang:

Christmas, golden feast of money.
When the profit pours like honey!
Forget the wishes, throw them out,
One less thing to worry 'bout.
Surely happy little children
Are really not our aim,
Children don't have any money,
So the parents are our game.
Spend a fortune on the presents,
So we tell them every day,
Or the love of your sweet children
Will on Christmas melt away!
Yes, their love will melt like snowflakes
Underneath your Christmas tree,
Only Gerold Goblynch's presents
Grant their love eternalleeeeheeeeyy!

With a big grin Rufflebeard bowed in front of Ben and then dropped onto his bottom, slightly short of breath.

"Th-that's a horrible song," Ben stuttered.

"They're playing that all the time in Goblynch's Christmas Palace in Yule Land," Niklas said. "It continuously blares out of the huge loudspeakers Gerold's Nutcrackers have installed all over the place."

"Tell him about the elves." Matilda's face had flushed an angry red. "Tell him what Gerold did to all the poor elves."

Niklas sighed. "That's the saddest part. Gerold has convinced most of the Santas that only humans can provide presents for human children. He persuaded them that elves were no longer up to the job."

"Slander!" the elves growled, and started hammering so angrily on the wheel that sparks flew up to the caravan's ceiling.

"One night," Niklas continued, "Gerold had his Nutcrackers drive all the elves out into the snow. Just like that. Nobody knows where they are. And now the Santas only deliver factory-made toys to the children."

"But some of us were smarter than greasy Goblynch!" Rufflebeard boasted. "And not all the Santas were convinced by his 'golden feast of Christmas,' so we persuaded them to let us hide in their coats."

"Just seven," Matilda said quietly. "And one of them was Niklas."

Niklas Goodfellow nodded. "Seven Santas against many hundreds — who all thought Gerold's Christmas was a wonderful thing. Seven who continued in secret doing what we had always done. The elves made our presents. The angels listened to the children's dreams and collected their wishes — the ones you cannot fulfill with money. And then the seven of us brought real Christmas presents to the children. At first, Gerold didn't notice anything. But then four Santas suddenly disappeared. Two others were dragged before the Great Christmas Council by Gerold's Nutcrackers and were slapped with a prohibition order forbidding them to carry out any Christmas work. Now they polish the Christmas Palace. Well . . ." Niklas took a deep breath. ". . . That left only me. Until that night just over a year ago when there was a knock on my door as well."

Ben had been listening so intently he had obviously almost forgotten to breathe. "What happened then?" he gasped, clearing his throat.

"This huge Nutcracker just took Niklas," Emmanuel said. "He grabbed him and dragged him to the Christmas Palace."

"We were so worried!" Matilda sobbed. "So we flew after him."

"And three of *us* hid in Niklas Goodfellow's pockets," Rufflebeard added. "Me, Firebeard, and Specklebeard."

"And then?" Ben looked at Niklas with big eyes.

The Santa shook his head sadly. "They put me on trial. The list of charges was longer than my arm. Gerold Goblynch had dictated it all himself."

"Un-Christmas-like behavior," Bugbeard listed. "Annoy-ing behavior toward parents, destruction of presents, loud and silly singing and dancing under a Christmas tree . . ."

". . . illegal employment of Christmas elves," Emmanuel continued, "conspiring with angels, continuous disobedience toward the Great Christmas Council."

"Yes, and the worst . . ." Niklas got up and poured the coffee dregs into the sink. "The worst charge was that I was unable to distinguish between nice children and naughty children. Most of the time" – he cleared his throat and looked rather sheepish – "most of the time I do tend to be nicer to the naughty children than to the well-behaved ones. It's always been like that with me."

"Some parents kept complaining about him." Bugbeard chuckled.

"But the children liked him," Matilda said, pouring Niklas some fresh coffee. "And how they liked him!"

"Not all of them." Niklas sighed. "Some were quite disappointed with my presents."

"Why?" asked Ben.

Rufflebeard somersaulted onto the top of the coffeepot. "Niklas didn't always bring the presents the little monsters had wished for."

"Would have been too boring!" Niklas smiled.

"The Great Christmas Council was not happy with that at all," said Emmanuel. "Niklas Goodfellow is full of quirks and surprises. They never knew what he would do next. And so they barred him from working as a Santa."

"For life," Niklas added quietly.

"Instead — he was supposed to enter orders into the database." Matilda beat her wings with indignation. "For the rest of his long, long Santa life."

"And so I stole Goblynch's reindeer, Twinklestar — the only one that hadn't been turned into salami — and fled." Niklas grinned. "They chased after me in their snowmobiles. A reindeer may not be as fast, but luckily for us it's a hundred times smarter than a snowmobile."

"They couldn't catch us!" Rufflebeard laughed. "That bunch of dopey lamebrains."

Niklas leaned back and sighed. "Not yet, my dear Rufflebeard, not *yet*."

Ben looked at him, deeply worried. "But what happens?" he asked. "I mean, what happens if they *do* catch you — these Nutcrackers?"

Niklas shifted uncomfortably in his chair.

"They turn him into a chocolate Santa!" Emmanuel whispered into Ben's ear.

"Nonsense!" Niklas called out. "All nonsense. I would make a miserable, scrawny chocolate Santa."

"And what happened to the other four? The ones that vanished?" Matilda was so excited, she had the hiccups. "Engelbert Firgreen and Sigmund Graybeard and Rupert Salix and Albert Sweet. Hmm?"

"Yes, yes," Niklas groaned.

"Eaten!" Rufflebeard croaked. "Tear off the wrapping, head off, eaten! And that's what's going to happen to you, Niklas, as soon as someone betrays you."

"Betray?" Ben choked on the gingerbread he'd just put into his mouth. "But who would . . . ?"

Niklas Goodfellow shrugged. "Other Santas. That's why I usually only work in areas that are of no interest to them, you know? Where parents don't order much because they don't have much money. The Great Christmas Council is not very strict in those areas. Here, though . . . I think you kids on this street get quite a lot of presents, don't you? And big ones, too — bicycles, PlayStations, huge dollhouses. Am I right?"

Ben stared into his mug . . . and nodded.

"That's what I thought." Niklas sighed. "That's why this is quite a dangerous street for me."

Everyone was silent.

Until Ben finally asked with a timid voice, "How much time do you . . . I mean . . . when will the other Santas get here?"

"If we're lucky they may have already collected their orders," Niklas replied. "That would give us until Christmas Eve. But if not . . ." He shook his head.

"Sometimes they do come back before Christmas Eve — to get the orders from the late deciders," Matilda whispered. "More and more people can't make up their minds what to give one another for Christmas."

A clock on the wall chimed eight times. A miniature Santa Claus came out, bowed, and vanished.

"Eight already?" Ben jumped up. "I have to go home."

"Pity." Niklas got up and showed him to the door.

"Can I — may I come back?" the boy asked, standing on the rotten stairs.

"Of course! We'll be looking forward to it," Niklas replied. "Isn't that right?"

"Yeah!" the elves shouted.

The angels waved, and even the carved wooden gnome and the grumpy-looking little nutcracker gave Ben a friendly nod.

Christmas Plans

Ben ran across the dark street and opened his garden gate. Before he went in, he cast a suspicious look down Misty Close, but everything was silent except for the rain. No snowmobiles appeared from the darkness, no gruesome Gerold Goblynch crept through the wet hedges, no giant Nutcrackers ground their big teeth at him. Only Niklas Goodfellow's caravan stood all by itself by the side of the road, small shadows moving behind the brightly lit windows.

Ben's parents were sitting in the living room, looking at travel brochures. Christmas in the sun. They'd been going on about it for weeks. And for weeks Ben had been trying to put them off the idea. He just hadn't been very successful. The only reason they hadn't booked the trip yet was because they couldn't decide where they wanted to go. Ben's mother wanted a small hotel; his father wanted a big one. Ben's mother wanted mountains; his father wanted the beach. Ben's mother wanted luxury; his father wanted a bargain. That's the way it always was. Ben's only hope was that by the time they came to a decision everything would be booked up. And he made sure that the brochures they were most interested in kept disappearing.

"Dinner's on the kitchen table," his mother called as Ben walked in. "Your father was just going to call Will and ask him how long it takes the two of you to solve one math problem. And did you see anybody at that strange caravan? Mrs. Heatherstraw told me she saw a man in a shabby red coat come out in the middle of the night."

"Hmm!" Ben mumbled, and went into the kitchen to get his food. Smoked fish — his dad's favorite. *I should have brought some of Matilda's gingerbread with me,* Ben thought. Smoked fish always made him burp.

***

"Well, I ask myself, what kind of a profession requires him to live in a caravan?" asked his father.

"Mrs. Heatherstraw says he is a scientist. A weather scientist," his mom said.

Ben almost choked on his smoked fish. He couldn't suppress a smile. "What are you smiling at?" His father watched him suspiciously. "Do you know something we don't?"

Ben didn't answer. His mother took the next brochure from the huge pile next to the couch. She lowered her voice. "Mrs. Heatherstraw says she heard several voices in there!"

Ben put another piece of smoked fish in his mouth. Matilda's gingerbread had definitely tasted so much better. "There's an elderly lady, too," Ben finally mumbled. It wasn't strictly a lie, after all.

"Don't speak with your mouth full," his father said. "An elderly lady? I suppose she's a weather scientist, too." He gave Ben's mother an amused glance.

"Well, they are in the Christmas business," Ben said — and instantly regretted his words.

"The Christmas business?" His mother looked at him in disbelief. Quickly Ben grabbed one of the travel brochures. Time to get their minds off that caravan.

"I'm not going," he said. "If you go away for Christmas, I'm staying here."

"Of course you can't stay here all alone," his father replied, smiling firmly.

"Ben, we've been through this a thousand times." His mother tossed one brochure on the table and grabbed the next one. "I don't want to hear any more about it. We just need to get away from it all for a bit."

Ben clenched his lips together. Curse it! He'd never liked Christmas. Spending Christmas Day in front of the television with his parents wasn't his idea of fun. But at least here he could go over to Will's if things got unbearable. That had saved him for years. And now, with Niklas Goodfellow out there and the angels and elves, maybe this year Christmas would be fun after all.

"What about Santa?" he asked, placing his half-eaten plate of fish on the brochures. "Will he go with us on vacation as well?"

"Ha-ha, very funny," his father replied. "And who gets angry with us each time we take him to visit Santa? You pulled the beard off the last one, remember?"

"That wasn't a real Santa!"

"A real Santa?" snapped his father. "OK, I'm tired of this conversation. As far as I'm aware, you have a math test tomorrow, right?"

Sometimes Ben wasn't sure whether his father knew the color of his son's hair, but he always knew what was going on at school.

"The math test'll be a breeze," Ben said. Then he turned and made his way upstairs.

"Oh, don't make such a face!" his mother called after him. "I am sure they have Santas at the seaside."

"Sure," mumbled Ben.

When he got to his room, he didn't switch on the light. He just sat down by the window and looked out on the dark garden and the wet roofs of the neighbors' houses. How he wished he could see Niklas Goodfellow's caravan from his room, and the warm light pouring out of the small window. Were the elves still fixing the wheels? And Niklas — was he still mending his worn-out coat? His boots were worn-out, too. *I'll get him a pair of Dad's,* Ben thought, *to make sure he doesn't freeze his toes off.*

Then he undressed and slipped into his cold bed.

Christmas Dreams

It was already after midnight when Niklas Goodfellow climbed out of his caravan. He had his two angels with him, an umbrella, and a small sack. The elves remained in the caravan, promising they would try once again to fix the second wheel. But they had yawned suspiciously often when they said so, and thrown longing glances at their bed-drawer.

The night was cold. Niklas's breath rose, cloud-white, from his mouth. A fine drizzle fell, freezing immediately on the pavement, and the thin ice crust shimmered beneath the streetlights. It was so slippery that the Santa's worn boots gave him hardly any grip. Skidding, he made it to the sidewalk, where he felt the frozen ground through his thin soles.

The houses on Misty Close were packed closely together, most of them large brick apartment buildings with several mailboxes by each front door, or single-story family homes with pointed roofs and pine trees in the front gardens. Very few windows were still lit. Niklas didn't ask the angels to fly to Ben's house — he wanted the boy to tell him his Christmas wishes himself. Instead he stopped in front of the next gate. "OK, let's get to work!" he whispered.

Hand in hand the two angels flew over to the house next door and peered through all the windows. Behind two of them they found sleeping children. Carefully the angels leaned their heads against the wet glass and listened to the children's dreams — while Niklas waited on the walkway, his feet getting colder and his nose redder. Every now and then he looked around uneasily, but the dark street was filled with nothing but silence. Even so, Niklas moved into the shadow of a high hedge until the light of the streetlamp touched only the very tips of his boots. Then, with frozen fingers, he pulled a golden notebook from his coat and wrote down the numbers of the houses.

"Niklas!" Matilda called. "Niklas, where are you?"

"Over here!" Niklas whispered back. "Behind the hedge."

The two angels landed on his shoulders.

"Two children," Matilda whispered into his right ear. "Kate and Sean. They want snow, and so many presents their little heads are all muddled."

Niklas Goodfellow nodded and wrote in his notebook: *Surprise.*

"Do you think they'd appreciate a little miracle?" he asked.

"I'm afraid not," Emmanuel whispered from his left shoulder.

Niklas wiped out his ear: Emmanuel always spat when he whispered.

"Fine," he sighed. "Let's keep going. Goodness, I really need a new pair of socks."

At the second house the angels simply shook their heads and fluttered straight on to the next one. Here they took ages, while Niklas waited in the freezing drizzle behind the garbage cans.

"Why don't you open your umbrella?" Matilda asked when they returned. "You'll catch your death in this horrid weather."

Niklas just shook his head – and sneezed three times. "Too dangerous," he sniffled. "I don't want to end up as a chocolate Santa just because of an umbrella. Now, please, your report."

"No children on the top or bottom floors," Emmanuel said, "but one girl on the middle floor – Charlotte."

"She has bad dreams," Matilda continued. "Poor thing. She wants snow and a better Christmas than last year."

"Ah!" Niklas scribbled it all into his notebook. "And what happened last year?"

"They moved," Emmanuel answered. "No friends, no Grandma, everything felt strange and she was very lonely. I think she still feels quite alone."

"Oh dear!" Niklas shook his head. "And how about a little Christmas miracle for Charlotte?"

"Worth a try," said Matilda, shaking out her wet wings. Emmanuel nodded.

So Niklas scribbled into his notebook: *Snow and an elf dance.*

"Snow, snow, snow," he said sadly. "They all want snow, but their little heads are running too hot with wishes. And on top of that our snow machine is broken – this really is going to be one sad Christmas!"

For many, many hours Niklas Goodfellow walked through the neighborhood with the angels in tow, taking notes. Here and there he tucked a few golden nuts or an apple under the doormat, or blew some silver dust from a small tin against a door frame, leaving little traces of Christmas.

When he finally returned to his caravan, Niklas was soaking wet and tired. Matilda and Emmanuel were drooped on his shoulders, their wings heavy from the rain and a long night's work.

Once more, before he climbed the creaky wooden steps, Niklas looked around. But still nothing stirred; the night remained quiet, and by the side of the road no silvery gray car lurked under the dripping wet trees.

That's how Gerold Goblynch sent his bad Santas into human cities — not on their snowmobiles, but in big silver-gray cars, each emblazoned with a bright silver star on its hood. No. No such car was anywhere to be seen, but sadly Niklas couldn't make out any signs of his reindeer, either — no tinkling of silver bells, no snorting, no cold wet nose trying to get into his coat pocket. How was he ever going to get away from here without Twinklestar?

The fire in the stove was just about to go out when Niklas finally opened the caravan door, but it was still wonderfully warm inside. A faint snoring rose from the elves' drawer. Of course, they were all fast asleep. The wheel was lying on the floor, the tiny hammers piled up next to it. A few spokes were fixed, but two were still broken.

"Oh those sluggards!" grumbled Matilda. "I've a good mind to wake them up."

"Let them sleep." Niklas took off his wet coat and hung it on a hook by the door. Then he poured the dregs of the coffee into a pot and put it on the stove. "Do you two want some?"

"No, thank you!" replied Matilda, yawning. "And it's not healthy for you, either, by the way." Then she flew up to join Emmanuel on the wardrobe. "Good night, Niklas!"

"Sleep tight, Matilda!"

The Santa let himself drop onto his bed, then pulled the damp woolen beard from his face. He felt both sad and happy. All those children's heads, hot from wishing, had made him sad. But if he thought of all the small surprises they would find tomorrow he was happy, very happy. *Tomorrow. Tomorrow I'll deal with the snow situation*, Niklas thought. *I'd be an embarrassment to my profession if I didn't manage to repair that silly snow machine.* He poured the hot coffee into his mug and warmed his fingers on it, listening to the tiny snores of the elves. *Life could be so wonderful,* he thought, taking one sip and another, till he felt himself slowly getting warm again. *Yes, sometimes it is really wonderful!* he thought. Then he carefully crawled into bed, keeping his boots on.

Two elves had made themselves comfortable on his pillow. Niklas got up again, carried them to their drawer, and placed them gently next to the others. Then he tiptoed back to his bed. *That boy,* he thought, pulling the blanket up to his nose, *didn't look happy at all. I should ask him tomorrow about his Christmas wishes. And poor Twinklestar, I wonder where he is. Probably wherever there's lots of marzipan.* And then, finally, Niklas Goodfellow fell asleep.

Ben Is Jealous

Ben was in an excellent mood as he walked out of school. Dean really *had* let him copy his math test, without complaining, and so for the very first time Ben had not just sat there, chewing his pencil, making unlucky guesses at the right numbers. He had even included two deliberate mistakes so as not to make it too suspicious. Well, even if it was suspicious, who cared? He strolled across the school yard, whistling, and decided not to go home right away. Why should he? His parents wouldn't be back from work before six, so he had plenty of time to visit Niklas Goodfellow.

Ben had to knock five times before Niklas finally opened the door. He was still in his pajamas, and yawning. The elves and the angels were also still asleep. A faint snoring echoed from every corner of the caravan.

"Ooops, sorry," Ben mumbled. "I thought . . . I mean . . ."

But Niklas smiled at him with delight.

"Oh, it's you! Come in, come in — before you turn the caravan into a fridge!"

Shyly Ben sat down on the same chair he had sat on before. Nothing had changed. Everything was just like the night before. Just as wonderful.

Niklas Goodfellow stared at his alarm clock. "What? Is that the time? Here we go again. Overslept. Well, it's not as if any of these lazybones were going to wake me."

"At school today," Ben said, looking around, "everyone was talking about some strange things."

"Indeed?" Niklas put the kettle on the stove. "Strange things?"

"Yes, golden nuts and . . . and glittering doormats and . . ." Ben pulled an apple from his jacket pocket. Where the stem should have been, it had a tiny Christmas tree. ". . . and things like this."

"Now will you look at that? Well, Christmas is certainly on its way," said Niklas. "Would you like some hot chocolate?"

Ben nodded and put the apple back into his pocket as carefully as if it were made of glass.

"I think I'll have tea for a change," Niklas said, dangling a tea bag into his mug. "Though I definitely feel like coffee — coffee, as black as a winter's night."

"They're all wondering . . . what you . . ." Ben cleared his throat. "What you're doing here. Our neighbor thinks you're a weather scientist."

"A weather scientist? Sounds excellent. What a good cover. I would have never thought of that."

Niklas raised his head. Outside there were voices — voices and a loud snuffling.

"Get away from there!" a girl's voice called out. "Get off, Mutt!"

"See? Even the dog thinks it's strange," a woman's voice said. "This run-down caravan suddenly appears out of nowhere. It makes the whole street look shabby. And the street sign — just look at what it did to the street sign."

Niklas peeped carefully out the window.

"There's a man in there," another voice said. "A tall, thin fellow. Someone should call the police."

The dog scratched at the caravan door.

Niklas quickly pulled his clothes on over his pajamas and boots, brushed his tousled hair, and splashed some water onto his sleepy face.

Then he gave Ben a conspiratorial wink and opened the door with a broad smile.

"A good day to you, ladies!" he said.

Ben looked past him. Mrs. Heatherstraw was standing in front of the caravan with the woman who owned the small shop at the corner and another woman Ben didn't know. Next to them stood a girl with a huge black-and-white dog. Mouseface. That's what everyone called her. She went to the same school as Ben and had been living in Misty Close for a little more than a year. How they all stared at Niklas!

"May I introduce myself?" the Santa continued. "My name is Niklas Goodfellow and I am a . . . um . . . weather scientist. I'm investigating the influence of certain street shapes on the weather, especially the Christmas weather. We . . . uh . . . we've been getting a bit worried about the extensive rain. Very worried. Well, have a nice day."

With a small bow Niklas tried to close his door again, but Mouseface's dog had stuck her nose in the way.

"Oh!" Niklas smiled at the girl. "Your dog seems to be interested in my research. Would you like to come in for a hot drink? As you can see" — he pointed at Ben, who had turned bright red — "I already have a visitor. The scientific skills of children are of particular interest to me, as children tend to be much more observant than adults."

Mouseface gave one of the women — apparently her mother — a questioning look.

"Of course, your mother is also most welcome," Niklas Goodfellow said. "I've just prepared some tea."

At that moment a miniature nutcracker stumbled between Niklas's legs and fell headlong down the steps.

Mouseface quickly picked him up, before her dog had the same thought.

"I still have some shopping to do, Charlotte," her mother said. "I could come and pick you up from here afterward if you like."

No, Ben thought. *Oh no.*

But Charlotte nodded, and her dog was already pulling her into the caravan. Mrs. Heatherstraw and the two other women were craning their necks, but Niklas closed the painted door in their faces with a firm smile.

With wide eyes, Mouseface looked around the caravan. Then she handed Niklas the nutcracker. "Here," she said. "I hope he's not broken."

Ben watched the two of them suspiciously. He didn't like girls, especially ones with big owl's eyes and hair as short as matchsticks.

Niklas placed the nutcracker on the table. "No, he's fine. Please, sit down," he said, pulling up another chair for his new guest. "What's your name?"

"Charlotte," the girl said, so softly that it was practically impossible to hear her.

"Charlotte. That's a nice name!" Niklas said, and prepared another mug of hot chocolate while Ben and Charlotte tried to ignore each other.

"Here you go," Niklas said, and pushed the two steaming mugs toward them. Ben took a sip and scalded his lips, but Charlotte suddenly just stared fixedly at the top of the wardrobe.

Matilda was sitting there, dangling her legs over the side.

"How lovely, Niklas, another visitor!" she piped. "Haven't you offered her a biscuit yet?"

And quickly the angel flew over to the shelf above the stove where she kept her biscuit tin.

Charlotte was so surprised that she spluttered hot chocolate all over herself and her dog.

Ben couldn't help smiling.

"Oh, I'm sorry, did Matilda startle you? Here." Niklas tossed her a towel and refilled her mug while Matilda came fluttering to the table with a big bowl full of biscuits.

"But I'm just a harmless old angel, my dear!" she chirped. "Just like the one up there."

Emmanuel peered sleepily over the edge of the wardrobe.

"Well, what do you say to that, Emmanuel?" Niklas brewed his tea and sat down at the table. "Two children! What a pity we have to leave. Although" — he sighed as he took a biscuit from the bowl — "our reindeer hasn't reappeared yet, and the wheel is still broken, so it may take a while. . . ."

"Reindeer?" asked Charlotte.

"Haven't you noticed? He's a Santa," Ben said without looking at her. "The weather story is just something he tells adults."

"He's a what?" Charlotte looked first at Ben, then at the two angels, and finally at Niklas Goodfellow.

"Yes, my dear, he really is a Santa," Matilda said, landing on Charlotte's shoulders with a familiarity that made Ben want to burst with envy. "And of course he also has a reindeer. Sadly, it keeps running away all the time, especially during thunderstorms. And since it is invisible, it's not that easy to find, you see."

"Oh!" Charlotte nodded.

She doesn't understand a thing, thought Ben. *I hope her mother finishes her shopping soon!* But what Mouseface said next made it worse.

"I bet my dog can find that reindeer," she said. "My dog has a very fine nose."

What? Was she crazy? Had she come just to make sure Niklas Goodfellow would leave again?

"But that's a wonderful idea!" Niklas exclaimed. "Would you really look for him?"

Charlotte gave him a shy smile. "I'd love to. I just need something for Mutt to get the reindeer's scent."

"The spare harness!" Matilda fluttered to the wardrobe. Ben's head filled up with the nastiest curses and swearwords. This wasn't fair. It just wasn't fair. *He* had found Niklas Goodfellow! Not this mouse of a girl, and now, if *she* found the reindeer, Niklas would leave!

"Ben, maybe you could help Charlotte?" Niklas looked at Ben expectantly.

"Oh yes!" Matilda clapped her hands. "We'll give them loads of marzipan. That silly animal is mad about marzipan!"

Mouseface smiled shyly in Ben's direction and then stared into her mug.

"Now this really could be our salvation!" Emmanuel sighed from the wardrobe. "Our salvation!"

Ben gave in. "OK," he grumbled. "I'll help her."

The Invisible Reindeer

Charlotte never saw the elves. They were still snoring in their drawer when her mother came to pick her up.

That at least made Ben feel a little better.

"In an hour's time. At the corner," Charlotte whispered before she left with her mother.

Ben nodded glumly — and sighed with relief when he was finally alone again with Niklas and the angels.

He helped Matilda and Emmanuel knead more dough and watched Niklas struggle to wake the elves. Then he sewed the tassel back on Niklas Goodfellow's hat. He was quite good at sewing. His mother had taught him, because he tore off his buttons all the time.

"You don't like Charlotte, am I right?" Niklas asked as Ben was threading the needle.

Ben pricked his finger in surprise.

"Why not?" Niklas asked. "She has beautiful dreams, you know. Beautiful ones, and terrible ones as well."

Ben had no idea what that had to do with anything. "She's a girl," he muttered, and made a knot in the thread.

"Ah!" Niklas said. "So? Matilda is also a girl."

"That's different," Ben replied.

"Ah!" Niklas repeated. Then he looked thoughtfully out the window.

Ben was ten minutes late getting to the meeting place. On his way out of the caravan he had run into Will — of all people — and had told him a big lie. What else could he do? Tell his best friend that he was meeting Mouseface to catch an invisible reindeer? Unfortunately Ben always stuttered when he lied, and Will knew that, so he was offended as well. How much worse could this day get?

Charlotte was already waiting for him, shifting from one foot to the other to keep warm. Her dog was jumping around her, wrapping its leash around her legs.

"Hi," said Ben, scratching the dog behind her ears. He

would have loved to have a dog, but his parents wouldn't allow it. "All that hair," his mother always said, "and they keep licking everyone and everything. No, you can have an aquarium. How about that?" But Ben didn't want fish. You can't cuddle a fish.

"Have you got the harness?" Mouseface asked him.

Ben nodded. He pulled the leather straps from his pocket and held them in front of the dog's nose.

Mutt sniffed at them curiously, but then she stuffed her nose into Ben's coat pocket. That's where all the marzipan was.

Charlotte laughed. "Hey, get out of there. That's not for you!" She pulled the dog back and handed Ben the leash. "Do you want to hold her?"

"Thanks," Ben mumbled, taking the leash. It was a good feeling.

Charlotte took the reindeer harness and held it under Mutt's nose once again.

"Go! Seek!" she said.

And that's what Mutt did. Sniffling and snuffling, her nose always close to the ground, the dog dragged Ben from street to street. Charlotte could hardly keep up with them. "That reindeer really must stink deliciously!" she called.

Ben just nodded. He felt wonderful. He could have run through the streets with Mutt for hours, days, weeks, forever. Even Mouseface's company didn't spoil it. Ben had always thought that girls talked all the time, that they poured out words by the bucketload over everyone's heads. But Charlotte hardly said anything.

Side by side they hurried through the wintry streets, until Mutt suddenly turned into one of the big shopping centers. Then she headed straight toward the town's largest department store.

"Oh no!" Charlotte stopped. "Don't tell me the reindeer's gone in there."

Ben didn't like that thought, either, but Mutt was already at the big doors, trying to yank the children inside.

"What are we going to do now?" Charlotte asked. "We can't take Mutt inside, but how can we find the reindeer in there without her?"

Ben shrugged. "Maybe — maybe Twinklestar's going to find us? I mean, the marzipan?"

"I don't know . . ." Charlotte tied Mutt to a hook next to the entrance and patted her head. "That place is full of marzipan. How's the reindeer going to smell *us*?"

They looked at each other helplessly.

"I think we should just go in," Ben said finally.

They stroked Mutt good-bye and pushed into the crowds.

The store was one big crush. Ben and Charlotte shoved their way past bellies and bosoms, dodging bulging shopping bags and strollers with screaming babies. Exhausted, they finally reached the escalator to the basement level: groceries and sweets. Christmas music hung like syrup in the stuffy air, and there were Santas and angels with glittery hair everywhere. Ben stumbled off the escalator and ran into a huge plastic Christmas tree.

"Can't you look where you're going?" a sales assistant barked at him.

Ben shot her a dark look and searched around for Charlotte. He couldn't spot her anywhere. *Well,* he thought, *not really surprising – small as she is.*

Suddenly something wet touched his hand. Wet and cold. He spun around, but there was nothing there. All he could see were crowds of tight-lipped people trying to reach the escalators and busy shoppers digging through the discount bins.

"Charlotte!" Ben stood on his toes and tried to pick her out. Someone pushed him in the back so hard that he nearly fell on his face.

Angrily he spun around, but there was no one there – absolutely no one. In fact, people were giving Ben a wide berth, as if he were surrounded by an invisible fence.

Invisible! Some*thing* nibbled at his sleeve and tried to push into his coat pocket.

"Charlotte!" Ben shouted. "Charlotte!" He took a step backward – and saw the huge plastic Christmas tree start swaying dangerously, although he still stood more than a few feet away from it.

"Come here!" Ben whispered. He reached into the empty space in front of him. "Come on." His fingers touched soft fur and leather. Immediately he grabbed it.

"Ben?" Charlotte appeared from behind a mountain of gingerbread tins. "Have you got it?"

"Quick!" Ben called back. "I can't hold on."

The invisible reindeer struggled against Ben's grip.

Helplessly he stumbled after it, straight toward that blasted plastic tree. The thing started rocking like a real tree in a storm. Then it leaned to one side, and ornaments and tinsel began raining from the branches. People started screaming and the crowd scattered.

The sales assistant stomped toward Ben, fuming.

But he was still holding on, while Twinklestar was nearly pulling him over.

"Climb on his back!" Charlotte shouted. "Quick!"

And suddenly Ben saw her sitting above him in the air, waving him wildly toward her.

But before he could get to her, someone grabbed his arm.

"Got you, you little devil!" the sales assistant screamed. "Look at this tree. That's going to cost your parents a fortune!"

His parents! With a last desperate effort, Ben pulled himself free and reached for Charlotte's hand. The next moment he was sitting behind her on the back of the invisible reindeer. The assistant stared up at them, her mouth wide open.

"Ho!" cried Charlotte, and tugged at Twinklestar's bridle. "Ho! Ho! Ho!" The reindeer leaped into the air, nearly throwing the children off again. Then it reared up and vaulted over the crowd. As light as a feather it pranced through the air, ten feet above the tables and racks. Ben nearly hit his head on a huge neon angel that hung from the ceiling.

The excited voices underneath them had fallen silent. Only the loudspeakers were still blaring out their Christmas music. Men, women, and children gazed silently into the air as Ben and Charlotte floated through the Christmas decorations on the invisible reindeer.

Only when Twinklestar flew up the escalator was the spell finally broken.

"Great trick!" someone shouted.

"Do that again!" a child called.

But Ben and Charlotte had already vanished. Twinklestar had galloped through the door and landed on the pavement before anyone in the store had time to realize what was happening.

"You ride ahead!" Charlotte called, slipping from Twinklestar's back. "I'll get Mutt."

Twinklestar leaped forward again.

Ben looked back toward Charlotte and just managed to see her untie the madly barking dog before the reindeer began cantering down the next side street.

"Whoa!" Ben cried, pulling the reins with all his might. "Stop! Stop, I said."

Much to his surprise, Twinklestar did indeed slow down, and stopped with a snort in front of a big hedge.

Without letting go of the reins, Ben slipped down to the

ground. "See what I've got!" He pulled the remaining marzipan from his pocket and held it in the air.

That was how he coaxed Twinklestar to the next lamppost. With trembling fingers he tied the invisible reins to it. Done! He looked around nervously. Luckily the reindeer had landed him in a very small side street. There was no one to be seen.

"Boy, oh boy!" Ben moaned. Exhausted, he leaned against the lamppost and closed his eyes.

A few minutes later Charlotte came running down the road with Mutt. "Have you still got it?" she panted.

Ben nodded. "Tied to the lamppost. It's trying to eat my jacket."

Charlotte gave him a relieved smile. "We handled that quite well, didn't we?"

"We did!" said Ben. And they smiled at each other. Proudly. Then they untied Twinklestar and made their way back to the caravan. Back to Niklas Goodfellow.

Santa's Workshop

Niklas?"

Nobody answered when Ben knocked on the caravan door.

"Maybe he's gone for a walk," Charlotte suggested. "Or don't Santas do that?"

Twinklestar was nibbling at Charlotte's hair again. She pushed his wet nose away and looked around. Niklas Goodfellow was nowhere to be seen. Only a fat man, loaded with shopping bags, was struggling down the street. Before Charlotte knew what was happening he had bumped straight into Twinklestar's furry bottom.

"Humph!" he said, and dropped all his bags and packages. He looked around, flabbergasted, but the only suspicious things in sight were the two children.

Charlotte yanked on the reindeer's harness. "Quick, let's go inside!" she hissed at Ben. "That man's already giving us very funny looks."

It was completely dark inside the caravan when Ben

opened the painted door. Only one little candle burned on the table. Next to it stood Niklas's coffee mug. But there was no sign of the Santa himself. The door of the wardrobe on which the angels usually sat was ajar, and a slim ray of light fell across the worn carpet. Ben cast a worried glance toward the White Door, but it was still firmly locked. "Strange," he mumbled.

Charlotte climbed into the caravan, yanking at the reindeer's reins. "That man's still staring!" she whispered. "Come on, Twinklestar! Please!"

Ben came to her aid. The reindeer resisted, and they heard its hooves slip on the stairs, but then finally it squeezed through the door — and became visible. His fur was as white as milk, his nose covered in marzipan, and his antlers festooned with Christmas decorations from the department store.

"Oh look!" Charlotte breathed. "Isn't he beautiful?"

"Hmm." Twinklestar licked Ben's nose. "But I wonder if he's allowed inside."

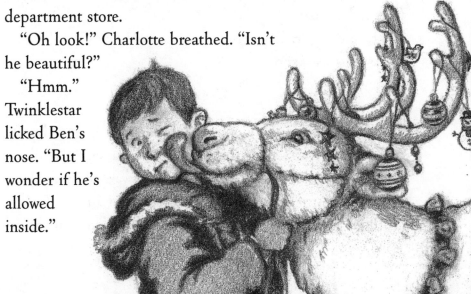

Charlotte flushed. "I . . . I thought at least this way he can't run away again."

Ben shrugged and looked around.

"There really is no one here at all!" Charlotte said, surprised.

"That's what I said." Ben pushed Twinklestar's hairy bottom out of the way and walked over to the open wardrobe. Strange sounds came from inside: tiny voices, little hammers, and the pattering of small feet.

"Do you hear that?" Charlotte whispered.

Ben nodded and cautiously peered through the crack. The inside of the wardrobe was brightly lit.

"What can you see?" Charlotte asked, but Ben didn't answer. What he saw would have left anybody speechless. Charlotte peered over his shoulder — and was as dumbfounded as Ben.

The old wardrobe was the entrance to Niklas Goodfellow's Christmas workshop.

⚓

The room behind the wardrobe doors wasn't large — hardly bigger than the rest of the caravan. But it glittered like a treasure chest. It smelled of glue and beeswax, and there were toys, lots of tiny, amazing toys, piled right up to the red ceiling. The toys were stacked on shelves, in wooden chests,

and in baskets. Some hung from the ceiling in big nets while others simply floated through the room on small carpets the size of handkerchiefs. The whole place was lit by candles, hundreds of candles, which illuminated the workbenches of the elves. There were lots more elves, so many more than the ones Ben had seen so far. Most of them were hammering, filing, sawing. Others were standing on the shelves, wrapping the tiny toys in silk paper, or piling up the finished ones to make space for more.

Niklas Goodfellow, in his threadbare Santa coat, was sitting in the middle of all the commotion. He was leaning over a rickety table writing in a small notebook. On a shelf above him, a seven-armed candelabra dripped wax into his hair and Matilda and Emmanuel were sitting on his shoulders.

Who knows how long the two children would have stood there, gazing with hungry eyes at the scene in front of them, if Twinklestar hadn't licked Ben's nose again.

Ben sneezed so loudly that the angels fluttered up from Niklas's shoulders in fright. Niklas spun around and the elves dropped their hammers.

"Oh, it's just the children!" Matilda exclaimed with relief. The fear immediately vanished from all their faces. The elves continued hammering, and Niklas waved at Ben and Charlotte cheerfully. Matilda fluttered over to them.

"Well, you really made us jump!" she twittered. "Everybody knows that the big Nutcrackers sneeze when they smell a real Santa."

"The big Nutcrackers?" Charlotte asked.

"Just forget it, my child!" Matilda replied hastily. "Even talking about them brings nothing but bad luck. Come in! Welcome to Santa's workshop."

The angel looked around with pride. "Isn't it all just splendid? I can hardly believe all this was built by these silly little men."

"Oi!" one of the elves shouted. "Careful what you're saying now, angel!"

"Real gnomes!" Charlotte whispered. "Real, living gnomes!"

"Those are actually Christmas elves," Ben said. He grabbed Twinklestar's reins. "Look, Niklas, we brought someone with us."

Twinklestar struggled, but with their combined strength the children managed to drag him through the wardrobe doors and into the workshop.

"Twinklestar, Twinklestar!" Shaking his head, Niklas put his arm around the reindeer's neck. "Look at the state of you! Your love of marzipan is going to be the end of you one day — and of us as well. Why can't you get that into your furry head?"

The reindeer gave Niklas a shove with his nose. Then he snorted and licked his hairy lips.

"Yes, and now you're trying to get into my good book again!" Niklas said. "But thanks to you we're up to our necks in trouble. Next time we fly into a storm, just come into the caravan instead of bolting off into the clouds like that."

"Or *we'll* turn you into reindeer salami, that's a Christmas elf's promise!" Rufflebeard shouted, slamming his hammer onto the workbench.

"Someone knocked on the White Door today," Matilda whispered to the children. "Three times!" Her voice trembled.

Ben looked anxiously at Niklas.

"What white door?" Charlotte asked.

But Niklas just put a finger to his lips and gently led the children over to one of the shelves. "Matilda, give Twinklestar some hay, will you?"

"What? As a reward for running away? Really, Niklas!"

Matilda scolded. "He's getting far too fat, anyway. Nearly as round as his previous owner." But obediently she flew to a big sack and returned with a big bundle of hay. "There!" she said, throwing it in front of Twinklestar. "I wish Niklas had left you with Gruesome Goblynch. The two of you were the perfect match!"

The reindeer snapped at Matilda with his big yellow teeth.

"Did you see that, Niklas?" she shrieked. "Did you see? He's sneaky, that's what he is. Is that the proper kind of behavior for Santa's reindeer? No!"

"Then stop insulting him," Niklas said. "After all, it's not his fault he was Gerold's reindeer once."

"And who is this Gerold?" Charlotte whispered into Ben's ear.

"He's the Stealer of Christmas!" Ben whispered back. For once he felt that he had found just the right word. Charlotte, however, looked as puzzled as before.

"Enough!" Niklas called out. "Enough of this unpleasant topic." He took the candelabra from the shelf and waved the children toward him. "Come on, let's have a look at some Christmas toys."

Little Secrets

Well, what do you think? Aren't my elves true wizards?" Niklas could hardly suppress the pride in his voice as he stood with the children in front of the shelves lining the walls of the workshop. Red candles burned on little silver stars, shedding their light on countless gifts, most of them not much bigger than a walnut.

Ben could only nod as the flickering light fell on cars the size of fingernails, dolls no bigger than acorns, insect-sized cuddly toys, and puppet theaters that were no higher than Ben's thumb. There were music boxes, trains, and magic things the children had never seen before. They were all miraculously wonderful, but tiny — so tiny that the children didn't dare touch a thing for fear of breaking the miniature gifts.

Charlotte asked the question that was on Ben's mind

as well. "But how are you supposed to play with these?"

"Ha-ha, they don't get it!" Goldbeard, the master ribbon binder, croaked. He dropped the huge red ribbon he had just turned into a giant bow and marched over to them. As nimbly as a squirrel he climbed the shelf, until he was level with the children's eyes.

"Stinky glue and scratchy sawdust, you humans are such ignoramuses!" he said. "Have you never asked yourselves how Santa manages to get all those presents into his sack? Huh? Never crossed your mind, has it? By normal standards

that blasted sack would have to be at least as big as Niklas Goodfellow's stinking caravan."

"Goldbeard, for once can't you at least try to express yourself in a more civilized manner?" Niklas scolded, although he could hardly hide his smile.

"Whatever," replied the elf, and did a handstand. "Of course, nothing's normal when it comes to Santas."

"The way you're explaining it," Matilda shouted down from Niklas's shoulder, "the poor dears are not going to understand a single thing!" With a serious face she fluttered over to Goldbeard, who was still doing his handstand, pushed him over, and sat down in his place. The elf tumbled off the shelf and landed in Niklas's outstretched hand.

"As you see, these toys are now just the right size for Santa's sack," Matilda explained, "but . . ."

"I already told them all that!" Goldbeard interrupted huffily.

"But," Matilda continued as if she hadn't heard him, "when Niklas takes them out of the sack . . ."

"Zappy-doodle-doo!" Goldbeard croaked, doing a somersault on Niklas's hand. "They grow."

Now it was Matilda's turn to get huffy. But the children finally understood what this was all about.

"Could you — I mean, could you show us how it works?" Ben asked.

Niklas smiled and sat Goldbeard amongst his ribbons again. Then he carefully took one of the tiny bicycles from the shelf — and touched it with his fingertip. The next moment, a shiny, full-size bike stood on the sawdust-covered floor of the workshop.

Lost for words, Ben and Charlotte stroked the red saddle and the chrome handlebars — until Niklas touched the bicycle again with his fingertip and in a flash the tiny, fragile machine was back in his hand.

"May I?" asked Ben.

Niklas nodded.

Carefully, very carefully, Ben took the miraculous object into his hand and stroked the silver spokes, which were once again as thin as a fly's legs.

"That's something, isn't it?" Goldbeard shouted from his workbench. "Only Christmas elves can build something like that."

"Show-off!" muttered Matilda, while Ben touched the tiny pedal. It turned.

"*Real* Christmas presents from a *real* Santa have another secret," Niklas said, "one that's probably even more important than the first one."

"*Another* secret?" Charlotte took a toy grocery shop, the size of a school eraser, from the shelf. She opened one of the drawers. It was filled with sweets as teensy as poppy seeds. Charlotte looked at Niklas, enchanted.

"If a child doesn't like a *real* Christmas present," Niklas answered, "the toy disappears into thin air."

"With a sigh!" Matilda added.

The children exchanged a worried look, but the miniature miracles in their hands were still there.

"That's never happened to any of my presents," Charlotte said.

Niklas shook his head. "Well, you wouldn't even notice it. It simply wouldn't be there, you see? But" — he put the candelabra back on the shelf and took both children by the hand — "real Christmas presents have become just as rare as real Christmas elves, or milk-white reindeer, or real Christmas snow. You've probably never seen one."

He walked with the children to the wardrobe door and they climbed back into the caravan. Mutt followed them, trailing her leash, and Niklas closed the door after her.

Suddenly the room fell silent: No hammering or shuffling

could be heard anymore. Only a faint smell of glue and beeswax lingered.

"I'm afraid I have to send you back home now," Niklas said. "It's quite late, and I still have lots of things to prepare for my second Christmas round."

"Can't we come with you?" Charlotte asked.

Niklas shook his head. "Oh no, I'm afraid that's not possible. A few Christmas secrets must remain just that — secrets!"

"Oh!" Charlotte sighed. She picked up Mutt's leash and realized she was still holding the toy grocery shop. She put it on Niklas Goodfellow's table with a guilty look. Hesitantly Ben put his hand into his coat pocket and placed the tiny bicycle next to it.

"No reason to be sad!" Niklas said. "Christmas is not far off. But I do hope you don't really want those. I prefer to give children surprises, you know!"

"I don't mind," said Charlotte. "Your presents are all wonderful."

"Well, thank you!" Niklas gave a bow. "I will pass that on to the elves. And should I, for any reason, no longer be here on Christmas Day, remember to leave your window open. Someone will bring you a present from me — that's a Santa promise."

The two children looked at each other.

"OK then . . ." Ben opened the caravan door, but stopped on the top step.

"At least you've got your reindeer back now," he said.

Niklas nodded. "Yes, and I think I haven't thanked you properly, have I?"

"That's . . . that's not what I meant," Ben stammered. "I mean — did the elves fix your wheels as well?"

Niklas nodded again.

Ben didn't dare to ask the next question, but Niklas answered it, anyway.

"I will stay for a while yet," he said. "Just a little while."

Ben was so relieved he nearly fell off the steps. Charlotte stood behind him, a bit puzzled. Of course. She didn't know anything about Gerold Goblynch and Niklas's secret life.

"Good night, Niklas!" Ben said. On the bottom step he turned around once more. "Do you think we're going to have snow soon?"

Niklas listened to the night. "Difficult," he said. "Do you hear all that noise? So many cars. Normally snow makes its own silence, but with all that warmth welling up . . . I don't know. If I had my snow machine, maybe, but sadly it took quite a beating during our crash. I am sorry. . . ." He shrugged sympathetically. "I'm sure the elves will manage to repair it, but even with the machine there is only one way of making the snow really fall, and that's risky, very risky. Well, we'll

see." Niklas ruffled Ben's hair. "Take care, you two. See you tomorrow, if you want."

He waved once more, and then the caravan door closed behind him.

Ben and Charlotte stood on the pavement, looking a little lost.

"Ben?" Charlotte finally said, fiddling with her earlobe.

"Yes?" Ben looked toward his parents' house. There was a light on in the kitchen.

"Why did Niklas say he'd stay just a little while? It's still quite a long time until Christmas." Charlotte pulled Mutt off the road.

"And who's this Gerold? And all that talk of sneezing nutcrackers and white doors." She gave Ben a pleading look. "Can't you explain it to me?"

Ben shrugged. They had reached his gate. "I don't know," he said, and pushed open the frozen gate.

Charlotte flushed bright red.

"And why not?" she asked crossly.

"Because!" Ben stopped and fished his keys out of his coat pocket. Then he turned around once more. "I'd just get it all confused, you know? I'm really not any good at explaining." Ben Lead-tongue. Wordless Ben.

Charlotte looked at him. "I would understand. I'm sure I would."

Ben put the key into the lock. Mutt sniffed at the trash can.

"OK," Ben said and unlocked the door. "Come on in, then. I'll try."

A Silver-Gray Limousine

Nice children," said Niklas after Ben and Charlotte had left. He got the coffee jar from the shelf and put the kettle on the stove.

"You drink too much coffee," Matilda observed. She and Emmanuel were sitting amicably with the elves on the table, sipping hot elderberry juice.

"What did you say?" Niklas asked absentmindedly.

"You drink too much coffee!" Matilda repeated. "I've told you a hundred times already."

"Yes, yes, you're right." Niklas pushed back his hair and frowned.

The two angels exchanged anxious glances. "Are you worried about Goblynch?" Emmanuel asked.

"Well, I'm worried about a lot of things."

Niklas sighed. The kettle gave a long shriek and spat its whistle against his chest.

"Ouch!" He took the hissing kettle from the fire and poured water onto the coffee. "You don't have to look at me like that. I know that we have to get away from here." He lowered his voice. "Do you think I haven't heard it? There. Again." They all listened, sudden fear on their faces. There was a knock on the White Door. Someone sneezed, and a creaky laugh came from the other side. "Goodfellow!" a hollow voice whispered. "We'll catch you soon enough."

"A Nutcracker!" Matilda breathed. Her eyes were wide open with panic.

"Wood-heads! Huh!" Cheesebeard, the fattest of all the elves, spat on the table in disgust. "We're not scared of them. Not us!"

"Right!" said Goatbeard, although he didn't sound very convinced.

Matilda shuddered, though, and Emmanuel stared at the White Door as if it might spring open at any moment.

"Steaming reindeer droppings! It's really high time to go, Niklas!" Rufflebeard burped and took another biscuit. "Why don't we leave tonight? Everything is ready, isn't it?"

"No!" Niklas shook his head. "No, we'll stay a little while longer. What would I tell those two kids?"

"You won't be able to tell them anything after Gerold's Nutcrackers have finished with you!" Specklebeard spluttered. The elf really was living up to his name, and now it wasn't only his beard that was covered with elderberry juice.

"Stop it!" Matilda moaned. "I'm worried sick with all this talk."

Niklas dug into his pocket and produced a small telescope — a special elf-made telescope. When he extended it, it became as long as his arm. "Emmanuel, would you mind opening the roof for me?"

The portly angel fluttered up to the ceiling and pushed open a vent. Through it a patch of night sky sparkling with stars became visible.

Niklas pointed his telescope toward it. "Hmm!" he muttered. "Hmmm . . . mm . . . mm."

"Mmmm-mmmm!" Cheesebeard giggled. "I get it."

"Oh, come on, tell us, Niklas!" Matilda cried. She landed on Niklas Goodfellow's head. "What do the stars tell you?"

"Please, Matilda, get off!" said Niklas. "My shoulders anytime, but not my head."

Offended, Matilda fluttered back to the table.

"The sun is far away, very far," Niklas said in a low voice. "Her steps are very faint. The longest night is not far off." He wiped the lens of the telescope and peered through it once more. "The stars are in our favor," he muttered, "very much in our favor. But . . . there's the possibility of a little trouble."

"A little trouble? Ha!" The smallest of the elves, Fleabeard, jumped up and laughed. "Well, we'd better be prepared, boys. Come on, back to work." One after another they climbed down the legs of the table and made for the wardrobe door. "Have you had a look at the snow machine?" Niklas called after them.

"All fixed," Specklebeard called back. "There were just two fiddly cogs broken."

With that the elves were gone.

"Emmanuel, you can close the vent again." Niklas got up and put some ashes from the stove into a little tin. "You know, Matilda, I think we should give Ben and Charlotte a little special surprise tonight."

"Oh no. You're not thinking about the polar glowworms?" Emmanuel crossed his eyes.

"It'll take us at least three nights to catch them all again!" Matilda fussed.

"And they're a dead giveaway," Emmanuel added. He sounded rather worried. "If one of Goblynch's Santas sees them, they'll know immediately where we are."

"I don't care!" declared Niklas. "I'm not going to lose all the fun of Christmas because of that beast Goblynch!"

"If you say so. You're the Santa here," Matilda replied pertly, and fetched a lovely wooden chest from the wardrobe.

Niklas, Matilda, and Emmanuel set off around midnight.

"Thank heavens at least I'm not going to get wet feet this time," said Niklas as he mounted Twinklestar.

It was a beautiful clear night, and the cold air bit into Niklas Goodfellow's nose. The reindeer carried him up to the tops of the trees as silently as a wisp of smoke, while Matilda and Emmanuel once again went from window to window to collect children's dreams. Niklas flew first to the front of Ben's house, and sprinkled some glowworms into the bare bushes lining the stony path from the gate to the door. Then he made Twinklestar carry him over the gabled roof.

"Right! Go right!" Niklas called, hauling on the reindeer's reins, but as usual Twinklestar couldn't resist diving through the smoke that rose from the chimney.

"Oh blast!" Niklas rubbed his stinging eyes. He coughed so hard that he nearly fell off the reindeer's back. "How often do I have to tell you? Santas are allergic to smoke, even if everyone believes we come down chimneys!"

Twinklestar's only reply was a vault through the air. Then he flew down into the bare garden behind Ben's house and landed on the lawn, next to a spindly tree Ben's mother had planted years before. While the reindeer licked the soot from his invisible legs, Niklas, coughing and sputtering, dismounted and looked around.

"Depressing," he muttered. He took the special tin with the ashes from his sack and sprinkled a bit on the lawn and the roots of the tree. Then he opened the chest with the glowworms and, humming a little Christmas tune, scattered the glowing animals over the bare branches. Satisfied, he inspected his work. Then he jumped back onto Twinklestar's back.

"Five roofs down, please!" he whispered into the animal's pointed ear. "But don't you dare try jumping over any more chimneys or there will be no marzipan for a fortnight. Understood?"

Twinklestar snorted defiantly and rose into the air. They left the glittering garden behind and flew toward Charlotte's house, which lay surrounded by old trees.

"Oh, this is easy!" Niklas tipped the chest and the rest of the polar glowworms rained down like silvery snow onto the branches.

"Now *this* is how I like my Santa work!" Niklas laughed. "All right, back to the angels, Twinklestar. But first we'll ride along the entire street once more."

The reindeer stretched its long legs and carried him down to the ground. Then it trotted leisurely along Misty Close, up on the left side and back on the right. As they passed the houses, Niklas popped pinecones into the mailboxes, sprinkled ash from the Christmas fire onto the doormats, and hung red apples on the shadowy tree branches — just within reach of children's hands.

The angels were already waiting on the gate of number 1.

"Phew, we're frozen through!" Matilda moaned, rubbing her ample behind. "Where have you been?"

"I told you to put on more clothes!" Niklas said. "Look at Emmanuel. He's wearing his coat."

"Oh, that silly coat," Matilda muttered. "Angels look stupid in coats. Anyway, the hood always knocks off my halo."

"Well, stop moaning, then." Niklas opened his notebook and pulled a pen from underneath his hood. "So, what did you hear?"

Emmanuel opened his mouth — and shut it again immediately. Through the quiet night they could hear the sound of a car engine, low and humming strangely. It was coming closer. Scared, the angels fluttered into Niklas Goodfellow's lap. "It's them!" Emmanuel whispered agitatedly. His round face was completely white. Matilda pressed her hands to her mouth.

Niklas steered his reindeer to the next gate. "Jump, Twinklestar!" he whispered.

The reindeer leaped over the gate in one bound, and the riders hid behind the high hedge.

The car drew closer.

"Go on, you two!" Niklas hissed at the angels. "See who it is."

The two angels took each other's hands and fluttered to the top of the hedge. Cautiously they peered over it.

A large silver-gray car purred along Misty Close like a stalking cat. When it reached Niklas's caravan, it stopped for a few endless minutes, its engine idling, before creeping off into the darkness again. The sound of the engine, though, was still audible for a painfully long time.

Pale and shivering, the angels returned to Niklas Goodfellow.

"Oh dear, oh dear!" wailed Matilda, wringing her little hands. "Oh dear, Niklas!"

"It was one of Goblynch's bad Santas!" Emmanuel's voice was trembling. "A huge silver limousine with pinecones on the license plate and a star on the hood. No doubt about it, Niklas, they've found us."

"We have to leave, now!" Matilda cried. "Or you will lose your head — and more."

"Nonsense!" Niklas steered Twinklestar back onto the street. "He probably didn't even see the caravan between all those trees."

"No!" Matilda exclaimed. "The car stopped right next to it."

"Did anybody get out?" Niklas asked.

The angels shook their heads.

"So you don't know if there was a Nutcracker with him?"

"Heavens!" Matilda threw up her hands. "You mean there might have been one of those horrible creatures in there? Heavens! Heavens above!"

"I don't know," said Niklas. "I don't know anything anymore." He fell silent. Twinklestar trotted back to the caravan calmly, as if all this did not concern him.

"Niklas, you must hide!" Emmanuel said. "Please, let's leave!"

But Niklas remained silent.

Twinklestar stopped in front of the caravan and turned his head inquisitively toward him.

Without a word the Santa slid from the reindeer's back and climbed the steps. Only when he reached the door did he turn around. "We're staying!" he said. "At least for a day. And you're not to tell the children about the car, understood?"

"You're crazy, Niklas!" Matilda whispered.

"You always knew that!" he said quietly. Then he pulled Twinklestar into the caravan. The angels followed him with drooping wings.

Trouble

The next morning Ben was late for school. He just couldn't tear himself away from the glittering glowworms. It was only when his father began to back out of the garage that Ben was startled out of his daydream.

"Wake up, boy!" his father shouted out the car window. "School's not going to wait for you, you know."

With a jerk Ben turned around and walked out the gate. Of course his father hadn't noticed the glowworms. He never saw things like that. *Just as well*, Ben thought. *Niklas put them there just for me, anyway.*

He skidded happily down the icy pavement. But when he passed Charlotte's house he froze in his tracks. Niklas had given her glowworms, too! Jealousy bit off a huge chunk of his happiness.

Well, Santas are meant to be fair, he told himself. That thought comforted him, and he spent most of his history lesson drawing Santas and little fat angels on his desk. The next lesson was P.E., the only subject Ben was any good at. Then there was math. . . .

I'll be going to Niklas's soon, he told himself every five minutes, his eyes glued to the clock. When the bell finally rang, Ben's schoolbag was already packed and ready.

Outside the gate he ran straight into Dean. Dean had just been demonstrating to some other kids how their bumbling principal panted up the stairs.

"Hey, Pea-brain, where did your folks get that brilliant light show in your backyard?" he asked.

"From Santa!" Ben muttered. He wanted to push past them, but Dean stood in his way.

Ben was taller than Dean and stronger. And ever since first grade they hadn't been able to stand the sight of each other. But considering how bad he was at math, Ben couldn't afford to fight with the only math genius in the class. Copying tests was what kept Ben out of trouble in school, and Dean knew it.

"Oh, you don't still believe in Santa Claus, do you?" he asked, grinning. Dean was always grinning so that everybody could see his gold tooth. He was very proud of it.

"Yeah. So?" Ben scowled.

"Oh really? And why do *you* of all people get stars sprinkled over your yard? Do you know him personally?"

"You got it." Ben pushed him aside, but Dean held on to his jacket.

"Pea-brain knows Santa! Well, I never. Which one? The one from the street corner, or the one from the department store?"

"The real one," Ben growled. "Let me go."

Dean raised his eyebrows. The three other kids pricked up their ears.

"The real Santa! You mean the fat one with the beard who's always shouting, 'Ho, ho, ho' and is a bit dumb? That one?"

"He's not fat." This time the words came, although Ben didn't want them to. "He hasn't got a beard, and he's definitely not dumb."

"Wow, that was quite a speech by your standards." Dean looked around at his audience for approval. "Maybe you think your dad is Santa? I really should explain a few things to you."

Ben felt the anger boiling up in his head like a red-hot broth. Whenever that happened he couldn't think clearly and his tongue became so heavy that he wanted to spit it out.

"Stop talking like that!" he roared. "You'll see."

Dean smiled with deep satisfaction. They had gained quite an audience by now. "This is getting better by the minute. And what, exactly, will I see, may I ask?"

Ben had no reply. There was none. He would never take Dean to see Niklas or show him the angels and elves. Never. He'd rather have them all think he was an idiot.

"How about some snow?" said a girl's voice behind him. "How about it snowing so heavily that you won't be able to open your front door? Would that make you believe in Santa?" Charlotte was standing next to Ben, giving him a self-conscious smile.

"Hey, Mouseface. Since when do you cover Pea-brain's back?" Dean looked at them both scornfully. "Wait, you had stars in your garden, too! Does that mean you know Santa as well?"

Charlotte looked at Ben.

"Awww, look at them. They're a couple. Mouseface and Pea-brain — what a match!" Dean gave a low whistle. Ben had never been so close to hitting him.

"OK. How about a new bet, Pea-brain?" Dean stared at the sky. "I bet the big snow miracle will never happen. If I'm right and there is no snow, say, within the next five days, then" — a huge golden-toothed smile — "you have to carry me on your back, around the school yard, during lunch break while I call out, 'Santa Claus is dead.' If you win, I carry you, and I will shout whatever you like. And since I'm feeling generous, you can copy from me during our next test. Is that a bet?"

Ben didn't answer. His head was still filled with thick red soup.

"Aha!" Dean made a sarcastic face. "So he doesn't exist after all, your Santa, does he?" Sniggering, he slapped Ben on the shoulder. "Don't take it to heart. Most of us have known that since we were three."

"I accept," Ben growled, pushing Dean's hand away. "I mean, I'll take your bet."

Dean nodded, satisfied and obviously slightly surprised. "Pea-brain, I'm already looking forward to it. I mean — I m-m-mean . . ." He loved to imitate Ben. The audience giggled. "I mean — I mean to our little ride. See you. And say hello to Santa from me."

Laughing, Dean ran out of the school yard. Ben stayed behind, feeling a little lost. He sensed Charlotte looking at him.

"I shouldn't have said that about the snow," she said quietly. "Should I?"

Ben shrugged.

"I just wanted to help you with that . . . that . . ."

"Jerk," Ben muttered. "He's a jerk, but he's good at math."

They both walked out of the school yard and down Misty Close.

"Are you going to tell Niklas about the bet?" Charlotte asked.

"Don't know."

They both walked in silence until they stood in front of Charlotte's house.

"Would you like to come and visit me sometime?" she asked. "I still don't know that many children here."

"Maybe," Ben mumbled. How on earth could you play with a girl?

"I'll see you at the caravan later on," Charlotte said. "I have to study for a test first."

"See you later, then," replied Ben. Then he turned and ran off. He still wanted to find those boots his father never wore before going to Niklas Goodfellow's.

⚑

"Ben?" his mother called from upstairs as he walked in the door.

"I have to go out again!" Ben shouted back. Why was she home from work already? He yanked the boots out of the closet and wedged them under his arm.

"I left early," his mother called. "Terrible headache. Look on the dresser."

Ben went over to it and froze.

Three tickets lay on the dresser. He instantly felt as sick as if someone had punched him in the stomach. *Children are never asked*, he thought, *never. They just get carried off.*

"You'll enjoy it!" Ben's mother called from upstairs.

Niklas Goodfellow's glowworms glittered in front of the window. And there it was again, that red-hot anger. Ben clamped his eyes shut. His head was hammering. He stared at the dresser and kicked it as hard as he could.

"I — am — not — going!" he shouted. "I'll be ill. I'll break a leg. I'll get the plague."

Then he grabbed the boots and stormed out of the house.

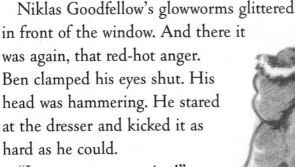

Another Crazy Idea

Ben's heart was still beating wildly when he knocked on Niklas Goodfellow's door.

"What's the matter with you?" Niklas asked as he let him in. "You're sort of white around the nose."

"Nothing," Ben muttered. "Here, these boots are for you."

"Oh, thank you!" Niklas said and looked at his own worn boots. "That's very nice of you, but I'm afraid they're no good to me. You see, every Santa wears special boots, made by elves. He wears the same pair all his life, and he never takes them off."

"Oh, OK . . ." Ben put the boots down.

"But do sit down!" Niklas went back to his chair. He was busy hanging bells on Twinklestar's harness. Ben sat by his side and found a biscuit to eat.

"No wonder the boy brings you new boots," Matilda called down from the wardrobe. The angels were tying ribbons. They were up to their round bellies in bows of all colors. "You don't look after your boots, Niklas. Just look at them!"

Embarrassed, Niklas bent down and wiped his sleeve over the dirty leather. "Yes, I know!" he admitted.

"It's dangerous for a Santa to take off his boots." Emmanuel was tying a thread of pearls around a red ribbon. "Did you know that, Ben?"

"Oh, don't go making up horror stories again," Niklas scolded.

"What horror stories?" Matilda asked boldly. "They're true, aren't they?" She leaned

forward confidentially. "As soon as a Santa loses his boots he turns into chocolate — within twenty-four seconds!"

"That's how Goblynch did it with the other four Santas," Emmanuel added sadly. "His Nutcrackers stole their boots and Gerold's now using them as candlesticks."

Ben shuddered. He stared at Niklas Goodfellow's boots again.

"As you can see I still have mine," Niklas said. "So let's stop all this gloomy talk. Why don't you tell us what you did all day?"

"Oh, nothing special." Ben looked out the window and up at the steel-gray sky. "About the snow . . ."

Niklas put his needle aside and cocked his head. "You'd like some snow, wouldn't you?"

Ben nodded.

"You know, as I said, there is a way, but . . ." Niklas shook his head.

"No, Niklas!" Matilda shouted. "No, no, no!"

". . . it would mean we'd have to open the White Door," Niklas continued. "There's plenty of snow behind it. We'd have to connect a pipe to the snow machine, connect that to the chimney, and feed the pipe through the White Door into the snow in Yule Land. Simple. That's how we used to do it. I mean, before Goblynch's Nutcrackers started patrolling Yule Land." Niklas had attached the last bell. He hung the harness on the wall.

"And if I . . ." Ben looked at him inquisitively. ". . . I mean, if I did it? If I went out there with the hose? The Nutcrackers only sneeze at Santas, don't they?"

"No, no, no, no!" cried Matilda. "What a crazy idea!"

"Not that crazy," Emmanuel said. "Gerold's Nutcrackers are only trained to spot Santas. They might not pay any attention to a human boy."

"That's a maybe!" Matilda shook her head firmly. "But what if they do?"

"They can't turn humans into chocolate," Emmanuel replied. "At least I don't think they can."

"You don't *think*?"

"I would like to try," Ben said. "Please. Can I?"

Niklas looked at him thoughtfully. "A little bit of snow is really that important to you?"

"It would . . ." He hung his head in embarrassment. "It would prove something."

"Prove what?"

"That Santa Claus really exists."

"Ahh. Would it prove that?"

Ben blushed. He nodded.

Niklas was still looking at him. But he asked no more.

"As you wish," was all he finally said. "But I won't let you go out there all by yourself."

Ben jumped up. "Be right back!" he called. "Thanks! Thanks tons!" – and he was out the caravan door.

"Crazy boy," Niklas murmured. "Such a crazy boy."

"Just as crazy as you," Matilda said from the wardrobe. "He'd make quite a good Santa."

Ten minutes later Ben was back – with Charlotte and Mutt.

"Great. Reinforcements!" Matilda sighed.

Niklas dragged the snow machine out of the workshop, together with a long red hose.

"You have to plunge the hose into the snow, up to this golden ring here," he explained to the children. "If we're lucky the snow will be high enough right by the door."

"And what if we're on the Great Christmas Lake?" Matilda asked tartly. "You know that the snow never lies very deep there."

"True," said Niklas. "But why should we be unlucky again? Fetch them two of the elf coats. And gloves. They'll definitely need gloves."

Clucking crossly, Matilda vanished

into the workshop. She returned with two tiny coats and gloves the size of pennies.

Niklas snapped his fingers and the things began to grow. "That's enough!" he called, snapping his fingers again. "Now, see if they fit."

They fit perfectly. The children pulled the hoods over their heads.

"Once you have put the hose into the snow you come right back to the caravan," Niklas told them. "Right away! Understood?"

The children nodded.

"The machine has to run for seven minutes," Niklas continued. "Then we can pull the hose back in and bolt the door again. Seven minutes."

"Seven minutes isn't much," Ben said.

"Seven minutes can be a very long time," Niklas answered, attaching the snow machine to the chimney. Then he unwound the hose and plugged one end into the snow machine. The other end he dragged to the White Door.

"Does the machine just blow the snow all over the town?" Charlotte asked.

Niklas smiled and shook his head. "No, it's a bit more mysterious than that. But the elves won't even tell me how it works. They guard the secret as fiercely as they guard their caps."

He put his ear to the door and waved the angels toward him. "Matilda, Emmanuel, could you listen as well, please?"

"I still think it's a stupid idea!" Matilda grumbled, but she put her ear to the door, anyway.

"I can't hear anything," Emmanuel said. "Can you, dear?"

Matilda shook her head. "No, but I still don't like it."

Ben looked at Charlotte. "Shall we?"

She nodded. Her face was nearly hidden under the big hood.

"Good." Niklas pulled a key from his pocket. "Emmanuel, please tell the elves in the workshop to be completely silent."

Emmanuel fluttered off. Matilda held Niklas back by his sleeve. "Don't do it, Niklas!" she said. "Anything could happen out there. This is no longer our Yule Land, but the empire of Gerold Geronimus Goblynch."

"Nonsense! This is still our Yule Land." Niklas yanked back the first bolt. "And it always will be. The children want snow, and snow is what they will get. It will be all right."

"Don't say I didn't warn you!" Matilda said, her voice shaking with fear.

But Niklas just shook his head and pulled back the second bolt. "Children have to keep believing in Santa Claus," he said. "And I am telling you, Matilda, if things carry on Goblynch's way, very soon no child will believe in Santa or in a real Christmas anymore."

With that he hauled back the third bolt. Then he carefully pulled out the elf boot stuffed in the keyhole and inserted the big key. He gave the children a last inquiring look.

"Open it," said Ben.

The lock creaked twice. Then the White Door sprang open.

Yule Land

A cold wind blew into the caravan. Snowflakes drifted in. Niklas opened the door a bit farther and poked out his head. Curious, the children peered beneath his arms.

All they saw was white and black. Thousands of snowflakes fell from a black sky. It was night in Yule Land.

"No tracks!" Niklas whispered. "Right, out you go."

Ben and Charlotte slipped underneath his arms and jumped out of the caravan. They immediately sank up to their ankles in snow. Thick flakes covered their coats, and within moments they were as white as the world around them. Ben looked around him. His eyes found nothing: no trees, no shrubs, no lit windows in the darkness. All he could make out were a few strange, pointy mountains in the distance. Mutt poked her head through Niklas Goodfellow's legs and howled.

"Sshh! You stay!" Charlotte hissed. "It's too cold for you."

"There!" Niklas cast Ben the end of the hose. He looked around worriedly. Ben yanked the hose a little farther out of the caravan and pushed it into the nearest snowdrift. It hit frozen ground long before the golden ring had touched the snow.

"Not deep enough!" Ben called. "Must be ice underneath."

"We're standing on the Great Christmas Lake, Niklas!" shrieked Matilda. "I knew it!"

"Bad luck and more bad luck!" Niklas moaned. He sneezed into the cold air.

"Call the children back inside!" Matilda shouted urgently. "Who knows how far we are from the shore!"

Niklas peered into the darkness with narrowed eyes. "She's right," he said. "Come back inside. It's too dangerous."

"No!" Ben took the hose and went on farther. Charlotte ran after him.

"Be careful!" Niklas shouted after them.

The children dragged the hose across the Great Christmas Lake, foot by foot. Charlotte tried to walk in Ben's boot prints as much as she could, staying close behind his back. She constantly had to wipe snowflakes from her eyes. The cold air chapped her face, but she still felt warm. *Without these elf coats we'd be icicles by now*, she thought, looking back over her shoulder. The hose of Niklas's snow machine snaked behind them and grew longer with every step — another elf miracle.

"It's so quiet!" Charlotte whispered. "Do you think it's always this still?"

Ben shrugged. "There." He pointed left. "There are reeds poking out of the snow. See?"

Charlotte nodded. "Yes, that's got to be the shore, and there are some really big snowdrifts behind it."

Ben trudged on. His legs were trembling with the exertion, but there was no time for a rest. Charlotte turned around again. Niklas's caravan was far away. There was a light above the door. Matilda had lit a lantern. As soon as they reached the reeds, their progress became even harder.

The hose got caught in the under-
growth, and Ben kept stumbling
over stones and branches
hidden beneath the snow.
Then the snow gradually
got deeper. When it
had reached their
knees, Ben stopped.

"Let's try again here," he said.

Charlotte looked around uneasily. Nothing disturbed the icy silence. Only her own heart was beating loudly in her ears.

"Those mountains there," she muttered, "they look strange somehow. Don't you think?"

Ben didn't answer. He was too busy trying to shove the hose deeper into the snow. Charlotte helped him, but kept looking around.

"It's deep enough here," Ben said.

"Quick!" Charlotte whispered. "I feel funny. As if someone is watching us."

"Nearly there!" Ben grunted. It was only a few more inches to the golden ring.

"Ben, there's something there!" Charlotte hissed. "Let's go back."

"Nonsense! There's nothing!" Ben pushed once more, and the golden ring disappeared beneath the top of the snow. "Done!" he said.

Suddenly, in the distance, Mutt barked and then howled like a wolf. It sounded eerie in the silence.

"I'm scared," Charlotte whispered.

Then, too late, they heard a creaking and cracking behind them.

Charlotte spun around and screamed.

Ben dropped the hose.

The pointy mountains were moving. The snow avalanched from them, and huge Nutcracker heads appeared from underneath. Their red mouths opened and closed. Their teeth crunched together and their wooden arms shook off the snow. Long legs in shiny boots rose into the air. Fixed eyes stared at the children.

"Run!" Charlotte screamed, pushing Ben forward.

And he ran. He ran for his life. He heard Charlotte panting behind him as his own steps crunched loudly through the snow. The lantern on Niklas Goodfellow's caravan bobbed up and down in front of him.

"Run!" They heard Niklas shout, too. "Come on, run!" Charlotte stumbled and fell into the snow. Ben pulled her up again, and they both jumped through the reeds. Gasping for breath, Ben leaped out onto the huge lake. He was a good runner, but Charlotte was falling farther and farther behind. The Nutcrackers stalked toward her on their stiff legs, the ice reverberating under their huge boots. Ben ran back to Charlotte and dragged her along with him.

"We won't make it!" she panted. "Let me go!"

Ben, wordlessly, just pulled her on.

The big steps came closer and closer.

But then there was another sound.

"Yahooo!" Niklas shouted. "Hoooh!"

His coat flying, a burning torch in his hands, Niklas galloped toward them over the ice. Here, in Yule Land, Twinklestar was far from invisible. Like white lightning he shot across the ice toward the two children. Niklas caught hold of first Ben and then Charlotte, and hauled them up onto Twinklestar's back.

The smell of a real Santa tickled the Nutcrackers' noses, and they began to sneeze terribly. But they didn't falter. They marched on, not missing a step, while their huge jaws made terrible snapping sounds.

"Away with you!" shouted Niklas, hurling his torch toward them. With a loud hiss, the flaming staff landed at the Nutcrackers' feet. But, incredibly, the fire, instead of going out, grew larger.

"The Christmas elves send their regards!" Niklas called. "This is a special present for you, shingle-heads!"

The Nutcrackers stopped dead.

Twinklestar, though, now spun around and flew back to the caravan. With a huge leap he jumped through the White Door, where ten elves were already waiting for them. With desperate haste they grabbed the hose and pulled it, bit by bit, back into the caravan.

"Was it outside for long enough? Was it seven minutes?" Ben asked breathlessly.

"Yes, the snow machine is running," cried Emmanuel. "Purring like a kitten."

"Oh, do hurry, for heaven's sake," Matilda called. "They're coming again."

The Nutcrackers had marched in a huge circle around Niklas Goodfellow's burning torch and now began approaching the caravan from two sides. One of them put his foot on the hose, but the elves yanked at it so strongly that the wooden giant lost his balance and fell headlong into the snow.

"Got him!" they shouted as one.

Immediately Emmanuel kicked the door shut with all his strength, and Matilda pushed the bolts across with trembling fingers and turned the key twice.

"The elf boot!" Niklas jumped from Twinklestar's back. "Quick, put it in the keyhole."

No sooner had Emmanuel stuck in the little boot than the Nutcrackers started hammering on the caravan.

"Goodfellow!" a voice boomed. "Niklas Goodfellow, come out of there!"

Nobody in the caravan even dared to breathe. They all stared, horror-struck, at the White Door.

"Goodfellow, we will get you!" a voice threatened. "You have contravened an edict from the Great Christmas Council. You are a Santa no longer."

That was the last straw for Niklas. "I am the *last* Santa!" he bellowed at the door. "The very last one, and I will remain just that. Did you hear me, you wooden numbskull?"

"Niklas!" Matilda squeaked. "Now you're starting to swear as well!"

But there was no stopping Niklas now. "Tell Goblynch that he will never catch me, even if he sends all his numb-skulls after me. He'll explode first, the disgraceful Christmas robber, corrupter of children's dreams, exploiter of angels, murderer of elves and reindeers!"

Exhausted, Niklas dropped into his chair.

"Oh, Niklas!" Matilda sighed. The elves and the children, however, were grinning broadly, and even Emmanuel smiled a little.

On the other side of the door everything went quiet. Terribly quiet.

"They're not leaving!" Charlotte quaked.

The four corners of the caravan started creaking ominously.

Then the whole thing started swaying dangerously from one side to the other. Children and elves fell all over one another. Twinklestar shied wildly, and the angels fluttered against the walls while Niklas held on to his snow machine.

"They're trying to knock us over!" Ben shouted.

"They won't manage it," Niklas called back. "We're firmly rooted in your world. They're just trying to scare us."

"Well, they're managing that quite well." Charlotte banged her head against a table leg and caught two cups that fell from the shelf. The old caravan creaked and cracked, but it held fast.

Finally the Nutcrackers had had enough. With a bang they set the caravan back on its wheels and stalked off. Everyone listened anxiously to their heavy steps getting farther and farther away. Only when there was nothing more to be heard, no creaking, no wooden cackling laughs, did they get up and look around.

Niklas sighed and picked up a broken wood carving. "A lot of work setting all this straight, friends. I don't even dare to look into the workshop."

"You lot wouldn't listen!" Matilda picked up the shards of her favorite bowl with a grim face. "You knew better!"

"Sorry!" mumbled Ben. Everything that had survived Niklas Goodfellow's crash landing was now broken as well: Niklas's coffeepot, most of the candlesticks, the tiny elf cups, and Matilda's angel china.

"We're terribly sorry," Charlotte said quietly. She was still sprawled on the floor. Snow was dripping from her elf coat.

"Nonsense, it's all my fault," answered Niklas. "I should have known better." He picked up a broken flowerpot. "But you know what? It was fun taunting those creatures, wasn't it?"

"Fun! You call that fun?" Matilda angrily held the remains of her teapot under his nose.

"But, Matilda!" Niklas stroked her hair with his fingertip. "This is angel china, it will grow together again. No, just remember those stupid faces when they stood in front of the elf torch." He chuckled. "That really was fun!"

"And the snow?" Charlotte asked. She pointed at the snow machine that was still humming quietly on the table. "We weren't outside long enough, were we?"

"Oh!" Niklas put an ear to the machine. "I think it might just be enough. We won't get ten feet of snow, but it will snow. Oh yes, it will snow tonight."

"Tonight?" Ben asked incredulously. After all the excitement he could hardly believe his luck.

Niklas nodded.

"Whoopeee!" Charlotte cried. She jumped up and danced around Twinklestar.

Ben, though, turned very silent. Yes, there would be snow, but he would soon have to fly with his parents to the sun.

Snow

Niklas was right. The next morning, at four o'clock, it began to snow. First there were only a few flakes, twirling to the ground. Then there were more and more, until they fell so densely that the air seemed to be made of snow. The roofs turned white, as well as the black branches, and even the gray pavement. The snow fell, and the world grew silent. When Ben got up at seven in the morning, the drifts were already nearly two feet thick. *Sledding*, thought Ben. *Snowball fights. Skating. Snowman building!* He skipped down the stairs, whistling to himself. It was impossible not to be happy surrounded by snow. Even though those wretched plane tickets were still lying on the dresser.

His parents, however, were definitely not in a good mood. "Blasted nuisance!" his father muttered, putting on his boots.

"Ben, come out with me. You've got to scrape the ice off the car while I shovel the driveway. Come on, I'm in a hurry."

"Yes . . . yes, all right!" With a frown Ben put on his clothes and stumbled outside. It was still snowing. Ben stopped in delight and let the soft flakes fall on his face.

"What are you doing?" shouted his father, clearing the snow from the driveway. "Have you frozen solid already? Sheesh, am I going to be happy to get away from here!"

Ben's good mood vanished as swiftly as the street under the snow. His face set into an angry grimace, he started scraping the windshield.

"Now will you look at that?" His father stood at the gate, the shovel like a weapon in his hands, and stared down the street. "They haven't even managed to clear the roads. Great! Next thing they're going to declare a state of emergency. How am I going to get to work?"

Ben giggled.

"Very funny!" His father threw the shovel to the ground. "And where did that tacky glittery stuff in the branches come from? Your mother really has the strangest ideas." He trudged over to the tree where Niklas had sprinkled the glowworms.

"Leave them alone!" Ben dropped the scraper, but his father was already reaching for the lowest branch. He shook it, and Niklas's glowworms flew off.

"No!" Ben held his father by the sleeve. "Stop it, they're mine!"

"Oh? Great! Then you can help me get them off. Even you should know that they could damage the tree. Do you want to buy a new one?" Ben's father pulled himself free of his son's grip. "What is this stuff, anyway?" Reaching up to the higher branches, he leaned forward, then suddenly lost his grip and slipped.

"Oouuuch!" he screamed. "My foot, darn it, my foot!"

Ben, frightened, kneeled next to his father as his mother came running out of the house.

"What happened?"

Ben's father ground his teeth. "I slipped."

"What? While you were shoveling the snow?"

"Of course not! Ask our wonderful son. Are you two going to help me up or do I have to freeze to death down here?"

Leaning on both of them, he hobbled back into the house and dropped onto the sofa, his face twisted in pain.

"Come on, Ben," said his mother, "make yourself a sandwich. You've got to get to school. I'd better find a way to get your father to the hospital."

"Is his leg broken?" Ben asked.

His mother shrugged. "Could just be a sprain. Anyway, they will probably have to put a cast on it or strap it up.

Which means" — she sighed — "good-bye, vacation. And Christmas in the cold."

Ben couldn't believe his ears.

"Oh, darn it!" he heard his father shout. "Darn it, darn it, darn it!"

But inside Ben a wave of happiness surged up. He could have sung, danced, exploded with joy. Although he did feel a touch ashamed of it.

His mother looked at him. "Well, you certainly don't look too disappointed," she said.

"Nope," muttered Ben and vanished into the kitchen.

The Wrong Santa

Niklas started from his sleep. Something had banged against his caravan. Yawning, he crawled out of bed and looked outside. A snowball hit the window, right in front of his nose.

Niklas smiled. Children were running across the snowy street, stretching their arms up to the falling flakes. Some were throwing snowballs at one another. Cars stood like frozen bugs in the driveways while their owners made their way to the bus stop. *There probably won't be any buses*, Niklas thought. A few adults were brushing the snow from their cars, but the flakes fell faster than they could clear them. Children snatched the scrapers from their parents' hands and ran off with them. *Brilliant!* Niklas thought.

He put the kettle on the stove, hummed a little tune, and climbed into his trousers. The snow machine was still purring quietly on the table, and from the workshop he could hear hammering . . . and swearing. Snow made the elves lively.

"Matilda, Emmanuel, get up!" Niklas called. He took a tin of gingerbread from the shelf, together with the only mug that had survived the crash and the attack of the Nutcrackers. The shards of the angel china had grown together again over-  night. Matilda's mug, however, now had two handles, while Emmanuel's had none. Niklas put them next to each other on the table. Then he wound up the music box. *Maybe we will have a proper Christmas after all*, he thought. *One should never give up hope.*

Two sleepy angels came fluttering to the table.

"Oh, is it still snowing?" Emmanuel put his nose to the window.

Niklas nodded. "Soon the whole world will be blanketed with snow. Listen! It's already much quieter."

"Oh wonderful!" Matilda sighed, fetching a jug from the shelf. "Then it was worth all the excitement. I nearly died of fear, I really did."

"But Matilda, angels can't die." Niklas poured water on the coffee.

"I said 'nearly'! Do leave some hot water for us, please?"

"Three more days," Niklas muttered. "Three days until Christmas Eve. The wheels are fixed, and the reindeer's back. Although, I admit, I would love to stay!"

Matilda was just about to answer when there was a fierce knocking on the door. All three jumped, but it was only Ben, who rushed in, breathless and shaking. "Niklas!" he panted. "Niklas, there's another Santa!"

Matilda dropped the jug in shock. It burst into a thousand pieces.

"Where?" Niklas asked.

"At the end of the street!" Ben gasped for air, and for words. "Charlotte is shadowing him." He dropped into a chair. "There are no other cars with all this snow. There's no school today, either. But, but . . . the snow doesn't seem to make any difference to this car. It's got such a funny thing on the front."

"Oh, oh, oh, oh! They've found us!" Matilda wrung her hands. "Now they're definitely going to take your boots, Niklas, and turn you into stale chocolate. And we will be turned into Christmas tree decorations. Oh dear, oh dearie me!"

"Matilda, stop it." Niklas walked over to the window and looked outside. There was no trace of the other Santa himself yet. However, his large silver-gray limousine was parked only a few yards away on the side of the street. Not a single snowflake stuck to it. They simply vanished as soon as they touched the metal.

"Here, my friend." Niklas put some freshly baked biscuits in front of Ben. "Do you want a hot chocolate with that?"

"You can't be thinking of making drinks at a time like this!" Matilda almost shouted. "Have you taken leave of all your Santa senses? We've got to leave, Niklas! Hitch up Twinklestar now, while we still have time!"

"No!" Niklas thumped his fist on the table. "Not this time! I will not sit in the woods on Christmas Eve, staring at a sackful of presents. No!"

"But what are you going to do?" Emmanuel asked quietly.

"Maybe we can find some tiny little street that Gerold isn't interested in," Matilda suggested, but Niklas just shook his head.

"I am staying right here," he said. "You can leave, if you want, but I am staying put. That's final! It's nice here, and I like the children, and . . ." Niklas looked out the window once more. ". . . I'm staying."

"You will do no such thing!" Matilda was outraged. "You are the last real Santa."

There was another knock on the door. Matilda fell silent.

"Hide, Niklas!" Emmanuel hastily pushed the Santa toward the wardrobe door. "Come on, let the boy open it."

Ben walked to the door while Niklas vanished into the workshop. The boy waited until the angels had disappeared as well. Then he carefully opened the door.

There he was, the other Santa, already standing on the topmost step. He seemed a little surprised to see Ben, but the next moment he was smiling down at him jovially. He looked as if he had climbed straight out of a picture book. His belly was round; his face was fat and friendly, with chubby cheeks, a knobbly nose above his white beard, and cheerful crinkles around his eyes. But not a single snowflake stuck to his shiny black boots. His long red coat had no patches, only shiny golden buttons and a white fur collar.

"Good morning, my boy," he boomed. "I would like to talk to the fake Santa."

"There's no Santa here," Ben replied. "What fake Santa?"

The fat Santa was still smiling, but his eyes glinted as cold as ice cubes. "My dear boy, don't lie to me. Don't you recognize the real Santa Claus when you see him?" he said, putting his hand on Ben's shoulder. It made Ben feel hot and cold at the same time.

"I am looking for a dangerous impostor, and I have a feeling you know where he is."

"Excuse me."

The Santa turned around. Charlotte was standing behind him. Ben had never been happier to see her. With determination she squeezed past the Santa's round belly, while he glared at her angrily.

"He was also at my parents'," she whispered into Ben's ear, giving the fat Santa an icy look. "What poor animal had to die for that?" she asked, poking his fur collar.

"Eh, what?" he asked. His sugary smile slipped a bit, but the next moment it was back, perfect and sticking to his lips like sweet honey. He was tall enough to look over the children's heads, and Ben noticed how hungrily he scanned Niklas Goodfellow's caravan. But when he didn't discover what he was looking for, his ice-cube eyes returned to the children.

"So what do you want for Christmas, boy?" he oozed.

"Don't know," Ben said.

"What?" The fat Santa looked at Ben with contempt. "Surely you want a brand-new games console? I can get it for you if you let me into this caravan."

"No." Ben tried to slam the door shut, but the gleaming Santa jammed his shiny boot in the door. He raised his gloved hand, and three more bad Santas jumped out of the gray limousine and ran toward Niklas Goodfellow's caravan.

Ben and Charlotte tried desperately to shut the door, but

the fat Santa pushed against it with all his weight. The other three were already coming up the steps. Suddenly Ben and Charlotte heard the wardrobe door fly open behind them.

"Get out!" Niklas shouted. "Out, Goblynch! And don't you dare touch those children."

"Goblynch!" Ben whispered.

"Yes, Goblynch!" the fat Santa boomed. He and his three henchmen brushed aside Niklas and the children and barged their way into the caravan. Two of them grabbed Niklas by the collar, and the third snatched the children, while Goblynch himself kicked the door shut.

"Let him go!" Matilda came flying from the wardrobe, red with rage. "Let him go, you horrible Christmas thieves!"

There was no sign of Emmanuel. The two Santas holding Niklas swatted at Matilda as if she were an annoying fly.

"An angel, yuck!" Goblynch snarled. "I bet you have elves, too." He walked over to the wardrobe and peered inside. Ben could hear the elves swearing. Goblynch slammed the door and locked it. "I'll deal with them later," he said, and walked back toward Niklas Goodfellow.

"My dear Niklas," he said in a voice as sweet as honey. "My dear, dear Niklas! How could you dare to disobey my ban? Playing Santa for years without permission, hmm? Shame on you! Look at him, children. Does he look like a real Santa? No, he does not."

Then he stroked his fat belly. "This is what a real Santa looks like."

"You scoundrel!" screeched Matilda as she pulled Goblynch's beard, but he ignored her.

"Gerold, you've always been an old windbag," Niklas said. "I'm not in the mood to listen to your blathering. So, shall we get it over with? But first let the children go."

"Oh no, let them watch what I do with rogue Santas," Goblynch replied with a nasty smile. "After that they can go home, as far as I am concerned, IF" — he held out his hand — "you give me the key to the White Door."

Niklas shrugged and pulled the key from his pocket.

Matilda collapsed, sobbing, on the table. There was still no sign of Emmanuel, even when

Goblynch stuffed the weeping Matilda into the drawer underneath the dresser.

"You rotten pig!" screamed Ben. He tried to struggle free, but Goblynch's henchman had him in a firm grip. Charlotte kicked his shin, but he just laughed.

"Wasn't easy to catch you, Niklas," Goblynch said as he walked toward the White Door. "You were more difficult than the other six. But I knew I'd get you all sooner or later." He pulled the elf boot from the keyhole and threw it over his shoulder. Then he unlocked the door. With a terrible grin he pulled back the three bolts. The children watched him, transfixed.

"Please feel free to step outside!" said Goblynch, tearing open the White Door. The stiff wind of Yule Land fluttered through his beard. "I'm afraid you're going to get cold, but this won't take long." Goblynch's fat belly wobbled as he laughed.

The Lost Boots

Goblynch's Santas shoved Niklas and the children out of the caravan. They all landed next to one another in the snow. It was dark in Yule Land, but it wasn't still snowing. The sky was clear and full of stars. Ben and Charlotte were freezing, but they tried not to show it. They didn't want to give Goblynch that satisfaction as well.

"Ah, what a wonderful night," he boomed. "Don't you
agree, Niklas? You know what? I will leave you as
a cautionary chocolate memorial here on the lake —
as a reminder to all the other Santas. Good idea,
don't you think?" He laughed out loud and
gave Niklas another shove.

A loud rumble came from the caravan.

"It seems your stupid elves can't wait for
me to deal with them." Goblynch gave his
Santas a signal. "Go on, throw him down,"
he growled. "Throw him down and take
off his boots."

"No!" Ben flailed wildly. "No!"

Then it happened. With a huge leap
Twinklestar jumped out of the caravan.
On his antlers sat Emmanuel and several
of the elves.

"Stop that animal!" Goblynch roared, but in that instant the reindeer knocked him flying. He plumped down into the snow with a groan. Surprised, his Santas let go of their prisoners.

"Niklas, over here!" Emmanuel called, and Niklas quickly swung himself onto Twinklestar's back.

"The boots!" Ben shouted.

Charlotte reacted immediately. They both jumped on Goblynch, who was still lying in the snow, waving his arms around helplessly. Ben grabbed the left boot, Charlotte the right. Then they both pulled.

"My boots!" Goblynch screamed. "My boots! Stop those brats! Now!"

His Santa henchmen stumbled toward the children.

"Throw!" Ben called to Charlotte.

Goblynch's boots sailed through the air. Niklas caught them as Twinklestar soared into the sky.

"Goblynch!" Niklas called, waving the boots. "Goblynch! You have twenty-four seconds."

"No!" Goblynch screamed. "I'll get you for this, Goodfellow!" Panting, he heaved himself up and stood in his red socks in the snow. "Give me your boots!" he barked at the nearest Santa. "Go on, hand them over."

But of course the Santa just ran away, as far as his

boots would carry him, all the way across the Great Christmas Lake. The other two looked at each other – then ran off after him.

"Nutcrackers!" Goblynch screamed. "Get them!"

Ben spun around. The Nutcrackers! He had completely forgotten about them. The huge wooden creatures were already thumping across the lake. There were five of them.

"Oh no!" Charlotte whispered, grabbing Ben's hand.

"Get their Santa boots!" Goblynch howled. "Their boots, you numbskulls."

But Niklas steered Twinklestar over one of the Nutcracker's heads and laughed out loud. "Your numbskulls are not going to help you now, Gerold. You've only got ten seconds left."

"Nine!" Charlotte screamed, throwing a snowball into Goblynch's face.

"Eight!" Ben yelled. His snowball hit the first Nutcracker right in the teeth.

"Seven!" Charlotte shouted.

Goblynch hopped from one stockinged foot to the other and tried to catch one of the children. But with his extra weight he wasn't very fast, and Ben and Charlotte just slipped through his fingers.

"Six — five — four!" Niklas shouted. He galloped past the Nutcrackers, so close that they lost their balance. Meanwhile the last of Goblynch's Santa henchmen slipped through the legs of the swaying giants and vanished forever into the darkness.

"Three!" Niklas yelled.

"You demon!" Goblynch's voice screeched with anger. "Give — me — my — boots!" He jumped up and down like a mad-man, trying to grab one of Twinklestar's legs. But instead he just dropped back into the snow like a sack of potatoes.

"Two!" Charlotte and Ben hardly felt the cold anymore. They were just staring at Goblynch.

"One!" Niklas landed with Twinklestar in the snow. "Zero!"

"Nutcrackers!" Gerold Geronimus Goblynch gasped. Then he shook his fists — and froze. A faint glitter covered his coat, his beard, his red socks. And then he turned brown — chocolate brown, from his head to the tip of his toes.

The Nutcrackers took one more step, waved their creaking arms, whirled around, and finally collapsed into the snow. Their huge heads hit the snow-covered ground just a few feet from the children.

Niklas climbed from Twinklestar's back and walked slowly over to Goblynch. Emmanuel followed him, his nose bright red and his wings shivering. Niklas put Goblynch's boots next to him in the snow.

"Has he really turned into chocolate?" Charlotte whispered, carefully stepping closer.

Niklas winked at her. "Do you want to try him?" He knocked on the big belly. It sounded hollow, just like a chocolate Santa.

Charlotte shook herself. "Horrible."

"His head was already hollow, anyway!" Specklebeard shouted. The elves were still perched on Twinklestar's antlers, happily dangling their legs.

"You're right." Niklas looked at Gerold's grim face thoughtfully.

"It hasn't improved his looks much," Emmanuel observed, and pinched Gerold's chocolate nose.

"Good-bye, Goblynch, you big bully," Niklas said. Then he put his arms around Ben and Charlotte and together they trudged happily back to the caravan, Twinklestar trotting after them. From outside they could already hear Matilda shouting. "Hey, let me out of here, you fat scoundrel!"

Ben was first into the caravan to free her.

"Where is Niklas?" she asked in a trembling voice.

"Here, Matilda." Niklas smiled and held his arms out toward her.

"Oh, you're still alive!" She landed on his shoulder with a sigh of relief. Then she looked around. "Where is that disgusting Goblynch?"

"Chocolate!" Thunderbeard crowed.

"What?" Matilda nearly fell off Niklas's arm. "How did you do it?"

"Well," murmured Niklas, gently pushing Twinklestar to one side. With a last glance at Goblynch and his Nut-crackers, he closed the White Door. "That's all thanks to one person alone!"

"Who?"

"Our dear Emmanuel."

Matilda, speechless, gazed at Emmanuel.

"Surprised?" Rufflebeard asked. "He waited until Goblynch was outside with the rest of you and then he unlocked the wardrobe door and let us out."

"You and Twinklestar," Niklas added.

"Yes, him, too," Dieselbeard grumbled. He sneezed into his beard. "Phew, by all the gluey sawdust of Yule Land, that was cold work."

"You know what?" Niklas clapped his hands. "I think we've got something to celebrate. Matilda, fetch your best biscuits, and you, Juicebeard, get us a keg of elf lemonade from the workshop."

"Niklas." Ben hardly dared to ask the question, but he just had to know. "Do you still have to leave? Before Christmas Day, I mean?"

Niklas scratched his ear and looked first at his angels and then at his elves.

"I don't know why I should," he said. "Can you think of a reason?"

"Oh, stop those stupid jokes," Matilda answered. "Of course we're staying."

Finally even Ben felt like celebrating.

No Christmas Spirit

Ben's father had a cast put on his leg. He was so angry that he actually nailed the airline tickets to the wall. The only thing that eased his mood was the B Ben got on his math test and his son's promise to do just as well on the next one. Of course Ben's father had no idea that Ben's improved math performance was only thanks to Santa Claus and two momentous bets.

And of course Ben also never told his parents anything about riding twice around the school yard on the back of the math-class genius, making him shout: "I believe in Santa Claus!" Dean had not shouted very loudly, but Ben had had a wonderful time nevertheless.

Since the mood at home was so bad, Ben spent the afternoons before Christmas Eve with Charlotte and Mutt. Mainly because of Mutt, of course. But also a little because of Charlotte. They built a whole gang of snowmen, went sledding together, and bought Christmas presents. With Charlotte, even shopping was fun. Will, who Ben usually spent all his time with, was mortally offended, and so they took him with them a few times. Most of the vacation, however, Will was left to throw gloomy glances at Charlotte.

Sadly, Niklas had placed the caravan strictly out-of-bounds for the children during those endless final days.

"We'll see one another on Christmas Day," he said in a friendly but firm voice, hustling Ben and Charlotte down the steps. Then he hung a sign on his door: DO NOT DISTURB (UNDER ANY CIRCUMSTANCES)! From then on, curtains with a pine tree pattern were drawn in front of the window all the time. Meanwhile a few polar glowworms twinkled on the caravan roof like fallen stars, and the smoke coming from Niklas's chimney sparkled silver with fairy dust. The whole caravan started to smell so deliciously of gingerbread and marzipan that even the people rushing past stopped and sniffed longingly.

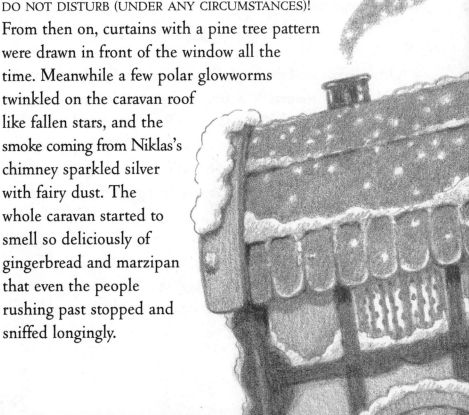

Ben sat by the kitchen window for hours every evening. He looked across the street and tried to imagine what was going on behind Niklas Goodfellow's glowing windows.

There were no Christmas smells at home — only the sharp scent of detergents. His mother, once she had realized they wouldn't be going south, had started cleaning the house. Ben borrowed Charlotte's incense sticks. He even snipped a few scented branches from the neighbor's pine tree and left them lying throughout the house, but that didn't help much. It still smelled like the household cleaning section of a supermarket.

On the twenty-fourth of December Ben's mother finally bought a Christmas tree. Ben wanted one in a pot, one that they could plant in the garden afterward. But his mother brought back a blue spruce that looked like a plastic tree and fitted exactly into Grandma's tree stand. "Come on, let's decorate it!" said his mother, bringing the box of decorations down from the attic. And with every bauble Ben hung on the spiky branches the scrawny tree looked a little more Christmassy. Usually his mother would interfere when they decorated the tree together. "No, that's too much tinsel!" or "Better put that ornament there, dear." But today she let him do whatever he liked. Only when Ben left the fat Santa that looked exactly like Goblynch in the box did she protest.

"But we always put him on the top. Why don't you like him all of a sudden?"

"He . . . he doesn't look real," said Ben, putting a small wooden angel on top instead.

"Not real?" His mother took the Santa from the box and held it under Ben's nose. "So what does a real Santa look like?"

"Well, different," Ben said.

His mother shook her head. "Ben, sometimes you do say the strangest things," she muttered. The Goblynch Santa, however, stayed in his box.

When the tree was finished, his mother put her arm around Ben and squeezed him. "Nice!" she said. "You'll see, it will be a wonderful Christmas — even without Santa."

When Christmas Day arrived it was wonderful. It started snowing in the morning. Ben emptied his

Christmas stocking onto his bed and smiled at the little joke-shop presents his mother found for his stocking every year. He knew there would be nothing from Niklas — he'd be seeing him later. When Ben came down for breakfast, his mother was lighting a few candles and she'd put a chocolate star on everybody's plate.

"Merry Christmas, Ben," she said.

Even his father managed a lopsided smile. He had tied a red ribbon around his plaster cast. The radio was playing Christmas tunes.

"What do you think?" Ben's mother took a roll. "Shall we open the big presents after lunch?"

Ben sighed. "As late as you like."

"Why?" his father asked. "Usually you can't wait."

Ben looked down at his plate. "Whenever Santa gets here."

"Oh dear, I had completely forgotten about him." Ben's father drummed on the table with his spoon. That usually meant: Caution! "Anyway, Ben, I think it's about time you stopped with that silly game. I know it's a messed-up Christmas, but you're not making it any better."

Ben said nothing. He poked his finger into his bread roll and pursed his lips.

"Oh, come on," his mother said. "It's Christmas! Let's have no fights today."

"We're not fighting!" Ben's father said. "I just want to

know why he keeps on with that silly Santa talk all the time."

The doorbell rang.

"I'll get it," Ben said.

It was Charlotte. Her hair was covered with snowflakes. Mutt gave Ben's knee a friendly shove with her nose.

"Merry Christmas!" Charlotte smiled awkwardly and handed Ben a little package. "Go on, open it."

"Thanks!" Ben stroked Mutt's big head. He was terribly embarrassed, because he had no present for Charlotte.

"Why don't you ask your girlfriend in?" Ben's mother asked.

"Thanks, but I have to get right back," Charlotte replied. "We have to pick up my aunt from the station."

"How nice! Well, Merry Christmas!"

"My aunt's not nice at all!" Charlotte whispered when Ben's mother had vanished into the kitchen again. "What do you think? When will he come?"

Ben shrugged. "When it's dark and he's finished his rounds."

"Oh dear!" Charlotte sighed. "A long time to go. Come on, unwrap it — I have to go."

Ben fumbled with the ribbon. When he finally ripped the paper apart, two pieces of chocolate-covered marzipan and a tiny plastic reindeer fell into his hands. Charlotte had tied bells to the antlers.

"As a souvenir," she whispered to Ben.

"Thanks!" Ben muttered. "I don't have . . ."

"It's OK," Charlotte interrupted him. "See you later, OK? And Merry Christmas."

"Merry Christmas." Ben followed her with his eyes as she stomped off through the snow. Then his gaze fell on Niklas Goodfellow's caravan. No sign of life there. Except for the silvery smoke that still rose out of the chimney.

This waiting is horrible, Ben thought.

He jumped when his mother tapped him on the shoulder.

"Where did you drift off to? Nice girl. But you can close the door now, it's getting cold in here." She stroked Ben's hair. "Come on, let's switch on the Christmas lights."

Ben's father hobbled in on his walking stick. The crutches the doctor had given him stood in the wardrobe, but he refused to use them.

"Pretty overloaded!" he observed, looking at the Christmas tree. Ben's mother shot him a look of warning.

"What time is it?" she asked.

"Twelve."

"Oh dear, that late already? I must check the oven!"

Ben's mother always cooked something "unusual" for Christmas dinner. His father loved that; Ben didn't. He didn't like unusual things, and he didn't like it when his mother spent most of Christmas Day in the kitchen while he had to hang around with his father. That could be quite hard work at the best of times — and usually made Ben flee to Will's on Christmas afternoon. But sadly Will was still offended because of Charlotte.

Ben's father dropped onto the sofa with a sigh. "How about a little game?"

Ben had been afraid of that question. His father liked games and especially quizzes. He called them general knowledge games and took them *very* seriously. He would lick his lips with delight before he took a card. And if Ben didn't know the answer, his father always had a long explanation in store for him.

No, Ben was definitely not in the mood for a game.

"I still have to wrap my presents," he said.

"Oh, doesn't Santa bring them?" his father teased. "OK,

pass me the remote, then. Maybe there's something interesting on the box for a change."

Ah well, it's still better than Christmas at the beach, Ben thought while he sat at his desk and wrapped first the car magazine for his father and then the cookbook for his mother. Outside, fat snowflakes were still falling from the sky. *Niklas, oh Niklas, when are you coming?*

Ben pulled Charlotte's present from his pocket. The marzipan was crushed, but it still tasted good. And the reindeer did indeed look a little like Twinklestar. Ben placed it under the vase of pine branches his mother had put on his desk. Then he looked out the window again, across the snow-covered gardens and white roofs. From the kitchen came the sound of clattering pots and Christmas music.

It's not a bad Christmas, Ben thought, *but it could still get a lot better.*

Santa Claus

They ate their way through three courses of Christmas lunch, and Niklas did not come. It grew dark. He did not come. They started giving one another their presents – no Niklas.

"Do you like your presents?" Ben's mother asked. She gave him a kiss. His father hummed a Christmas tune and looked at his car magazine.

"Great!" Ben pushed his new cars across the carpet. One after another vanished underneath the sofa.

"Even though Santa didn't bring them himself?" his father teased, laughing. Ben would have loved to kick his leg cast.

"You look sad," his mother said. She looked concerned. "Shall we go for a nice Christmas stroll in the snow? What do you think?"

Ben shook his head and turned away from her. Surely Niklas would still come. He simply had to come. Otherwise everything would have been for nothing, the Nutcrackers and Goblynch and everything.

His mother got up to gather the torn wrapping paper. She always started cleaning up right after the presents were unwrapped. But suddenly she looked up in surprise.

There was a knock on the front door.

"I'll get it!" Ben called. He stumbled over his presents and ran to the door. He was so excited, he hardly managed to turn the handle.

"Merry Christmas, my boy!" Niklas boomed, ringing a huge bell in his hand and making such a deep bow that his bushy beard nearly touched the doormat.

Ben smiled. He was so happy. So deliciously happy. He felt like bursting with happiness.

"Are you going to let me in?" Niklas asked, giving him a wink. "Even a Santa doesn't like to be left out in the cold."

"Of course!" Ben hastily stepped aside. Niklas looked wonderful, simply wonderful, with his cotton-wool beard and his red hood pulled over his dark hair. He had even polished his boots. His coat only had one tiny hole on the right elbow, and he was covered from head to toe in polar glowworms.

The huge sack on the young Santa's shoulder already looked nearly empty.

"I always keep the nicest kids until the end." Niklas stepped into the living room and made a small bow to Ben's parents. "A very Merry Christmas to you and congratulations on your wonderful son!"

"Merry Christmas!" Ben's mother nearly choked with surprise. His father didn't make a sound. He just sat there staring at Niklas as if he had just crawled out of the chimney.

Niklas Goodfellow let his sack drop onto the carpet and put his bell next to it. Frowning, he looked around the room. Then he went to the radio and switched it off. The blaring Christmas music vanished like a bad smell. Niklas put his finger to his lips and his hand in his coat pocket. When he pulled it out again, Emmanuel was sitting on his palm, a little lute in his hands. The plump little angel fluttered to the Christmas tree, sat on a branch, and began to play. Beautiful.

"Ben, could you please switch off the lights?" said Niklas, loosening the red ribbon from his sack.

Ben switched off the lamps and pulled the plug on the tree lights. The room fell into darkness. Only Niklas glittered and glimmered. He clapped his hands and the glowworms spread over the entire room. Emmanuel's lute sounded as cozy and soft as cotton wool.

"Good!" Niklas said, stroking his beard. "This is more like it! All ready for the presents?" He smiled mysteriously and looked into his sack. "Matilda, please bring out the gifts. The parents' first — in this exceptional case the parents also get something."

Matilda floated out of the sack, made an airborne curtsy, and fluttered toward Ben's speechless parents. She held a tiny present in each hand, tightly wrapped with a ribbon and a bell. "Merry Christmas!" she chirped, and let the presents drop into the adults' laps. Then she flew back to Niklas.

Ben's parents just sat there and stared at their gifts. All of a sudden they looked like children — like the children they had once been, many, many years ago.

"Angels!" Ben's mother whispered. She gently stroked the little package, the tiny bell, and the ribbon. Ben's father hid his present in his hands as if he was afraid Niklas was going to take it away again.

"And now for the most important person!" Niklas

announced. "For Ben, the scourge of the Nutcrackers, the enemy of all gruesome Santas."

Matilda flew back into the sack and came out with two packages. "Merry Christmas, Ben!" she called. Then she flew close to his ear and whispered, "At the caravan at midnight — to say good-bye."

Ben nodded. "Merry Christmas!"

He took the presents from the tiny angel's hands. Emmanuel plucked a few more chords on his lute, then he fluttered back to Niklas Goodfellow's shoulder.

Matilda sat down next to him.

"And a wonderful Christmas to you all," said Niklas. He stepped up close to each one of them in turn and tapped his fingers against the little packages. Gradually the presents began to grow.

Niklas stepped back with a smile. He tied up his sack and threw it over his shoulder. Then he walked slowly backward to the door. Only after he had reached the hallway did he clap his hands and call back the glowworms.

Then he strolled out into the night. The door shut softly, and Ben and his parents sat in darkness.

Ben's mother was the first to move. She felt her way into the kitchen and returned with two burning candles. She put them next to the Christmas tree. "Merry Christmas," she said, giving Ben and his father each a kiss. "Who's first?"

"You," said Ben.

With a timid smile she sat down on the sofa and pulled the ribbon from her package. She opened the rustling paper. On her lap lay a little music box with two small angels that looked very much like Matilda and Emmanuel. When Ben's mother carefully wound it up, they heard the same tune Emmanuel had played.

Enchanted, they all listened. Then Ben's father cleared his throat. "Is it my turn now?"

"Of course!" Ben grinned.

His father clumsily removed the ribbon and pushed the paper aside. There were three things inside: a pair of pink glasses, a book with the title *A Thousand Questions Without Answers*, and a small sled with a label that had illegible writing on it.

Ben's father put on the pink glasses and looked around.

"What do you see?" Ben asked.

"That's a secret," his father said, "between me and Santa." He looked at the label. "Ah, now I can read it. PLEASE LEAVE OUTSIDE. WILL GROW IN FALLING SNOW!"

Ben's father grabbed his walking stick, put Niklas Goodfellow's book without answers into his pocket, and hobbled with the small sled to the front door. "I hope it grows quickly!" he called over his shoulder. "And I hope Ben will pull me."

"Of course, Dad!" Ben said. His mother was still staring in amazement at her little music box.

"Now it's my turn!" Ben said.

"Oh yes, of course! Sorry!" his mother said. "Go on, I can't wait."

His father came back a little out of breath and dropped onto the carpet next to Ben. "Go on, Ben." He still had the pink glasses on his nose.

Ben first pulled the ribbon from the smaller of the two packages. The bells attached to it tinkled softly. Inside the paper was a little box covered with stars. Ben lifted the lid carefully. On a bed of sawdust lay a tiny flute, and next to it a wooden elf exactly the size of Niklas's Christmas elves.

"What kind of a strange fellow is that?" Ben's father asked.

"It's a Christmas elf," Ben answered. He blew into the little flute. With the first note the wooden elf started to move. He shook his stiff legs and frowned. Then he hopped through the sawdust, turned a few somersaults, and stuck out his tongue at Ben.

Ben took the flute from his lips and laughed. The little wooden fellow immediately froze.

Ben's father gave him a gentle shove. "Go on, make him dance again."

"No, open the second gift," his mother said.

Ben picked it up and turned the long package in his hands. Then he unwrapped it.

Inside was a nutcracker. It looked exactly like one of Gerold Goblynch's Nutcrackers.

"He looks spooky," his mother said.

Ben nodded and smiled.

His father gathered himself up. "I'm going to check on my sled. Want to come outside with me?"

They all put on warm clothes. It was still snowing.

"Whoopeee!" Ben's father yelled. "Look at that!"

The sled had already grown to the size of a brick. "If it carries on snowing like this we'll have a fully grown sled by tomorrow."

"Ben, darling" — his mother put her arm around his shoulders — "I don't know where you found this Santa Claus, but he's the most wonderful Santa I could ever imagine."

Ben shrugged. "That's because he's a real Santa, Mom." He paused. "And actually, he just fell to Earth."

Farewell, Niklas

It was ten minutes to midnight. Niklas Goodfellow was sitting on the stairs of his caravan, looking down snow-covered Misty Close. Everything was ready. Twinklestar was hitched up and waiting on the side of the street. Only a quiet snort every now and then betrayed him. The empty Christmas sack was stored safely in the wardrobe. The elves were snoring peacefully in their drawer. Matilda and Emmanuel were asleep under Niklas's hood. All that remained to be done was to bid the children farewell.

Niklas sighed and looked up at the sky. The weather would not play tricks on them tonight. The snow had stopped and, apart from the stars and the moon, the sky was clear and dark.

A garden gate squeaked, and Niklas saw Ben trudging across the street. Farther down, Charlotte was walking toward them with Mutt. The children's breath hung white and wet in the air. Both of them sat down on the steps next to Niklas.

"Well, you two? How did Santa Niklas do?" he asked.

"He did wonderfully!" Charlotte said and gave him a big kiss.

"Hey, who's kissing who out there?" Matilda asked, poking her head sleepily from Niklas's hood.

"And next year?" Ben asked. "I mean, will you be back next year?"

Niklas shrugged. "Maybe. Now that Goblynch has turned into chocolate I must look for new recruits. Maybe we can find a few real Santas. I can't do all the work myself, after all."

"Please, come back," Charlotte said.

Niklas gave her a wink. "All right. I promise." He yawned, and Emmanuel rolled out of his hood. Niklas caught him just in time.

"Sorry," Emmanuel mumbled. Then he curled up and went back to sleep in Niklas's hand.

"As you can see, we're all quite tired," Niklas said. Very carefully he slipped the angel into his coat pocket.

Matilda fluttered onto his shoulder and rubbed her eyes. "About time we found ourselves a nice, quiet cloud," she said. "I need to sleep for at least four weeks."

"Angels, elves, and Santas usually hibernate after Christmas Day," Niklas whispered to the children. He looked up at the sky and stood up. "Time to leave. Take care, you two. I hope you have a wonderful holiday!"

Ben and Charlotte got up, and Niklas hugged them tight. "I'll miss you," he said quietly. "You saved the last Santa, and who knows? Now perhaps Christmas will become magical again after all. Maybe you'd like to become my apprentice Santas in a few years' time?"

"Will I have to stick a beard on my face?" Charlotte asked.

Niklas laughed and checked Twinklestar's harness one last time. "I think so. You know, I also wanted to get rid of the beard. It itches and tickles terribly. But what can you do? A Santa without a beard would be even worse. I think it would confuse people too much."

They all stood together next to the caravan.

"Well, see you next year." Niklas Goodfellow climbed the steps. "See you again when the days are as short as socks and the nights as long as sleeves."

"See you!" Matilda called. She wiped a few tears from her cheeks.

"Bye," murmured Ben sadly.

"Remember your promise!" cried Charlotte.

Niklas waved at them once more and disappeared into the caravan. The old vehicle rumbled down the empty street, faster and faster, until it finally took off into the air.

"Until next year!" Charlotte whispered.

Mutt howled at the moon. And Ben knew he would be spending a whole year just waiting for Christmas.